Puppy Lve

L.T. Smith

Ylva

Foreword

I would like to thank you for buying this book. As a lover of animals, dogs especially, I have always dreamed of helping those less fortunate than I. In this case, it is help for what we all consider to be "Man's Best Friend". When I first penned *Puppy Love*, I always had the dream that if it was ever published, then all my royalties would go to help those pups in distress.

There are many reasons why an animal finds itself in difficulty. With the recession, many people are finding it hard to make ends meet and just feeding a family is stretching their meagre wages. Dogs, as it appears, are not the priority. I am not judging these people—luckily for me, I've never been in that situation. It is not only that people have to give up their pets, mostly with a heavy and broken heart, but the Trust also helps and cares for dogs that have been mistreated, unloved, and cast aside.

The aim of the Dogs Trust is to give stray and abandoned dogs a second chance at a brighter future with responsible, caring new owners. They are totally reliant on voluntary donations to continue the fantastic work they do. Without the help and support of people like you, it would be simply impossible to care for over 16,000 dogs every year.

Thank you, dear reader. With the purchase of this book you have helped to make a difference to our furry pals, and for that I will be forever thankful.

L.T. Smith—Linda to you.

Supporting www.dogstrust.org.uk
Registered charity 227523 & SC037843

Acknowledgements

Thank you, Astrid and Ylva Publishing, for making this dream come true. You have supported my dream to help a cause that is very important to me. As well as my royalties, you are giving part of your profit to another animal charity based in Germany. You are brilliant.

Day Petersen—you are wonderful. Thank you for polishing this novel to perfection. The pups thank you too. Lots of woofs and tail wagging for you.

Amanda Chron. You have made my man Mutley seem like a Lothario on the front of this book. He thanks you, and so do I. I should imagine he will get the ladies even more now. Shame he doesn't quite know what to do with them apart from chase and growl at them. Sounds like a plan... And thank you, too, for donating your fee to the Dog Trust.

Finally, I hope you, the reader, enjoy this book and recommend it to another animal lover, then another, and then another. That would mean loads of money going to a very good cause.

L.T. Smith

Dedication

To my men, Joxie and Mutz.
The canine version of "The Krays".

"WOOF!"
Ruffly translated...
"THANK YOU!"

Chapter One

January 2012. New Year's Day. Noon. Hangover. Every single one of my resolutions was already broken, and so was my cell phone. Seems that dropping it down the toilet, fishing it out, and then dropping it onto a tiled floor isn't the wisest course when it comes to technology. I would like to blame someone else for my stupidity, but it was all down to me trying to text my sister from the bathroom of Dixie's nightclub, to ask her to help me escape the blind date from hell. Seems I should've done it before I'd downed eight vodka and Cokes, but that would be hindsight, wouldn't it.

Rubbing my head and wincing, I stumbled from my bed and went to relieve my bladder. Sitting on the throne, I contemplated the mysteries of life. Do a person's fingers actually get fatter when one is inebriated? The previous evening, it had seemed as if each digit had spread over at least three keys on the keypad and ended up making a mish mosh of words—even if I had been in any shape to read them. Even though I was pissed and sporting the metaphorical beer goggles, I still couldn't muster up any

1

attraction for Cherie.

Don't get me wrong—Cherie wasn't a minger, as such, just...
just...shallow. Lazy and shallow. Stupid, lazy, and shallow. A
little like me, by the sounds of it. After all, here I am saying I
stumbled out of bed at noon, had buggered up my phone because
I was pissed and wanted to get away from someone because I
couldn't get pissed enough to shag her. Cherie could've been
my double.

Shower time. Sigh. The feeling of griminess from the club
began to wash away. It was replaced by more memories of the
previous night: Cherie trying to cop a feel at every opportunity,
and me dodging her tentacles at every one of those attempts like
I was on a firing range on target practice day. This brought on
more vigorous scrubbing and a pledge to never believe my sister
when she told me the woman she worked with was a catch, and
to not drink vodka and Coke ever, ever again.

Three o'clock saw me arriving at my sister's house feeling
a little more alive and ready to seek retribution. But when my
niece answered the door with her gap-toothed grin and eager-
ness to hug my legs, I decided the roasting over the coals could
wait a while longer.

"Happy New Year, Aunty Wellie. Me needs a kiss now." Lily
scrunched her eyes closed, puckered her lips, and waited for me
to plant one on her.

Instead, I grabbed her underneath her armpits and hoisted her
up. A yelp followed by excited screams shot from her mouth as I
frantically slapped kisses all over her face. "Gerroff!"

More squeals, followed by more kisses.

"You attacking my daughter?" Abbie's voice drifted down
the hallway.

I stopped trying to eat my niece and glared over the blonde

bunches on her head. "Go play, Lils. Aunty Ellie is going to kick Mummy's butt."

"But..."

"Yes. Mummy's butt. Go. Tell grumpy chops we leave in twenty minutes."

Whatever question Lily was going to ask next stayed unasked. What they were going to do was more important to her than being manhandled by her spinster aunt.

"DAAAAAAAAAAAAAAAAAAAAAAAAADDDDDDDD DDDDYYYY!" And she was gone, although the echo of her voice was still very much present.

"Want a cuppa?"

I glared at Abbie. I didn't want a cuppa; I wanted an explanation. Why had she thought I wanted to be set up with a woman who had more hands than a poker game and more one-liners than a nineteen-seventies stand-up comic, without the actual humour.

"Before you start getting all righteous, Cherie would be good for you."

"Fuck that."

"Lily, Elles, Lily." My sister was good at checking my bad language in front of my niece. Thankfully.

A voice from the living room demanded, "What?"

Both Abbie and I shouted, "Nothing, baby," and I continued to glare at my sister.

Abbie sighed and moved closer. "You need company, Elles. You spend most of your time either at work or working at home. Don't you want someone special in your life?"

Not like Cherie, I didn't. My shoulders sagged. I knew Abbie was only thinking of me, but I was big enough to look out for myself. If I wanted a relationship, I would get one, right? I was happy in my own little solitary world. I had my family, didn't I? My job? What else did I really need?

"It's been, what, eighteen months since your last girlfriend. Time to move on, hon."

Move on? I hadn't even wanted to go out with Tina. That, once again, had been a result of Abbie's interference. Tina was too needy, too ready to have the moving truck outside my door after the second date. Talk about the caricature of a lesbian relationship. I'm surprised she didn't order a turkey baster and a sperm donor from eBay as an early birthday present for me.

A surge of anger welled up inside me. "Stop, okay? Just stop with this, Abs. I am not a charity case who needs fixing up." Why couldn't people just accept that I was happy being on my own? What was the big deal about being tagged to someone else?

Abbie opened her mouth, but I cut her off. "Not everyone needs someone else to feel whole, okay?" I watched a hurt expression flit across her face, and even then I couldn't stop myself. "I don't need this, and I don't need you. I'm going." With that, I spun around and left my sister looking stunned.

I hadn't even made it to the car before I felt a hand on my thigh, tugging at my jeans.

"Where ya goin, Aunty Wellie?"

I turned and looked down.

Big green eyes were looking pleadingly up at me. "Mummy said you were comin' wif us today."

I opened my mouth to say I couldn't make it, you know, make excuses to a kid who believed I would not lie to her, but I couldn't do it.

"Me's gitin' a puppy."

A puppy? A spark ignited inside me that felt foreign, almost

4

like something people might classify as excitement.

"Mummy said you cud help pick her." Tears welled in the corners of her eyes, and I watched as one spilt over and trickled down her cheek. "If you dun't come, me won't get one."

Aw fuck.

Twenty minutes later, we were all bundled in my brother-in-law's car and heading to the local dog pound. Rob tried to get me chatting by pulling faces in the mirror and cracking bad jokes, but I was too busy giving my sister the silent treatment to fall for his antics. Lily didn't notice the tension in the atmosphere; she was too excited about getting a dog. Every time Abbie tried to make eye contact, I did the immature teen thing and hunched my body closer to the door and stared out of the car window with a "fuck the world" facial expression. Sometimes I surprise myself with my ability to be a knob.

When we pulled up in the car park at the Dogs Trust, I felt my flicker of excitement turn into a full blown raging flame. Stuff the melodramatics of trying to pretend I was angry at my sister. It would have been difficult to say who got out of the car more quickly, Lily or me.

Abbie approached me cautiously, her face trying to gauge how I would respond to her after my giving her the silent treatment. "Look, Elles. I'm sorry, okay?" She tilted her head to one side, her lips pursing in consternation. Moving closer, she whispered, "I...I won't do it again."

I squinted at her, and my expression showed my disbelief. "What was that, sis?" I loved to watch Abbie squirm.

She tutted before starting to say it again.

"Stop."

She did.

"I need to actually hear you promise me you will keep your

nose out of my business."

Another tut clicked off her tongue before she said, "I promise you, Ellie, I won't stick my nose into your life."

I grinned stupidly. "That'll do for me." I reached forward, grabbed hold of her and pulled her close. "Happy New Year, sis."

"And a Happy New Year to—"

"Come on! Me wants a puppy!" Lily was tugging on the door handle with all her might, trying to get inside the dog pound without us.

Laughing, I turned to look at Abbie and Rob, but was distracted by the arrival of a four-by- four entering the car park. The tyres scrunched over the gravel as the car spun to a stop. I don't know why I found it necessary to stare. I just felt that I couldn't pull my eyes away until I saw who was driving the car. Call it a totally fucked up moment.

The driver's door opened slowly, as if this was a cinematic shot on slow speed. The next frames showed a long, jean clad leg cupped at the calf by a brown leather boot, then a second leg.

I watched as the legs stretched even longer and met the ground. All the moisture seemed to evaporate from my mouth.

"Close your gob, Ellie." Abbie's voice sounded as if it was a million miles away, floating to me on wisps of wind or as a distant memory.

The legs moved away from the car door and made their way over to where we were standing. Those glorious legs seemed to get bigger, and my focus moved from the thighs to the hips, from the hips to a flat jumper-clothed stomach, and onwards and upwards to the gentle sway of an obviously female chest.

I blinked, as my subconscious must've realised it was rude to stare at a woman's chest, especially if you hadn't been formally introduced. So, on came the view of a slender throat, a strong jaw, a crooked smile, and the tip of a straight nose. My heart rate was ramping up, thumping wildly inside my chest as the anticipation of the whole picture seeped from my imagination.

"Afternoon."

Such a sweet voice. Heavenly. Angelic, yet laced with something that most definitely didn't denote harps and purity. With a snap, I shut my mouth, my teeth clattering together like castanets. I honestly believe I answered with an "afternoon" of my own, but I couldn't swear to it.

Then she was gone. Dark brown hair fluttered through the door and left me wanting. I hadn't seen her eyes. For some reason, I felt that I needed to see her eyes. Looking into someone's eyes allowed me to see so much. It wasn't just attraction that made me do it; I was like that with everyone. Shaking my head, I grinned stupidly. I turned to speak to my sister, but realised I was on my own. What the...

"You coming?" Rob was standing in the doorway, waiting for me. "Looks like the other ladies wanted to see another kind of puppy dog eyes."

Amazing to think he is just a builder and not a comedian, isn't it.

Once inside, I saw the back of the mysterious woman's head just in front of my sister. She was talking in low tones to one of the volunteers at the dog shelter, and I couldn't hear what she was saying. Believe me when I tell you I was really trying—and also attempting to see what she looked like, especially the colour of her eyes. If the rest of her body was any indication, they would be perfect as well.

"What is the matter with you?" Abbie hissed. "How much did you drink last night?"

I grunted, and my incomprehensible noise seemed to pique the interest of the mysterious long-legged, four-by-four driver in front of us. She turned her head slightly, and I almost got to see her face, but the woman she was talking to asked her something and recaptured her attention.

Then, she was gone, and I was left feeling as if I had missed out on something totally life changing. I was typically not one for being overly dramatic, although with my sister, I was not averse to melodrama. Nevertheless, I knew I had to see the woman in toto before I would be able to achieve some semblance of peace.

Ten minutes later, we were allowed through the doors and into the back where the dogs were housed. Seeing those adorable little faces nearly made me forget my quest, and I was acting exactly like Lily. Seeing her eyes wide, mouth open in wonder and inability to speak made me long for the days when the smell and excited licks of a dog were all it took to make the world seem right. For me, that had been a long, long time ago. After Toby died, I had promised myself that for as long as I had breath in my body, I would never allow myself to be absolutely smitten with a dog again. He was my first and last pet, my special boy, the lad who had taught me that getting covered in mud and other unmentionable things was one of the most special times a girl could have. My relationship with Toby was completely different from any friendships I'd ever had before him. Upon reflection, I guess I had been in love before, but hadn't allowed myself to remember loving Toby, because of the pain that came with it. It had taken me so long to get rid of the images of my loveable lad's last moments on this earth, that I couldn't open myself up to the possibility of losing someone that meant the world to me.

God. The trust, the absolute devotion he had shown, allowing me to slowly walk him into the room where the vet was waiting to end his pain. I still remember the way Toby looked at me, still remember the acceptance, the understanding. It hurts to think about the feel of his fur as I ran my fingers through it, loving the heat of his skin before the coldness would take over.

One injection. Toby had the time to look at me, lick my hand, and lie down as if he was just having a nap. I physically felt the crack inside my chest, the pain spreading like a plague and destroying every memory of happiness I had ever had.

Leaving him there all by himself was even harder. In my mind, he wasn't dead; he was sleeping. If I left, I would be leaving him alone to wake in a strange place and look for his mum. Hard. So fucking hard.

It was Abbie who had taken my hand and pulled me to her. Abbie who had held me as I sobbed over my loss. Abbie who had taken me home and stayed with me until I had cried myself to sleep. She had still been there for me when I woke and remembered what I had done. I felt as if I had murdered Toby. The part of my brain that told me it was the right thing to do wasn't very convincing.

"Hey, sis." Abbie's soft voice brought me out of the memory of the sad times. A tear had escaped without me knowing, and she leant forward and brushed it away. "You okay?"

I nodded and sniffed.

"If you would rather we leave—"

"Mummy! Look! She likes me." Lily was face to face with a Jack Russell who was frantically trying to lick her through the bars of the kennel.

How could I do that to my niece? Or to the Jack Russell, for that matter. The little mite was trying to get to Lily every which way she could.

"Nah, I'm fine." I ruffled Lily's hair, then tugged gently at a strand. "I'll just have a look around for a bit."

Abbie nodded and gave me a sympathetic smile.

During the time I had been conjuring memories of my little lad, I had forgotten about the woman who for a brief time had absorbed my focus. It wasn't until I walked to the far side of the kennels that the goal resurfaced. She was kneeling on the floor with her back to me. I could hear her talking to someone, her voice cooing and gentle.

I stepped to the side so I could see the object of her attention. A Border Terrier was bouncing in front of her, his tail wagging wildly, a ball stuck in his mouth. Something clicked inside my chest as I saw the life and joy in the little mass of black and tan, but it was nothing compared to how I felt when he turned his focus to me. Sparkling dark brown eyes absorbed me in one look, the tail stiffening before going crazy.

I didn't even realise I was kneeling until I felt the dog leap into my arms, the ball forgotten and a frantic tongue wiping away the remnants of my tears. I laughed, and the dog became even more intent on kissing me hello.

"Hey there, fella." More licking and mewling noises. "Want to play ball?"

"Yap!"

Over he went and recovered the discarded ball, then brought it straight back to me. Plunk. It hit the ground, and he used his nose to bat it closer to where I was kneeling.

"Yap!"

I snatched the ball and bounced it, laughing as the little furball tried to catch it.

"Charlie! Here, boy!"

That voice again—the one I'd heard only twice before but seemed to know already, forced my attention from the scrambling dog. Looking over, I saw the woman's face for the first time. Fuck. Yes, fuck. She was everything I'd hoped and more besides. My breath caught in my throat, and my heart was pounding so loudly that I would have sworn everyone in the room could hear it.

Charlie stopped his chasing and turned his head to the speaker, then to me, then to the woman again.

"Come on, fella!"

Okay. She was attractive. Granted, she had the voice of an angel. And true...those eyes, God, those eyes. Dark brown. Deep. Soulful. I was finding it difficult to split my attention between her and Charlie... But let's slow things down a minute. She wanted Charlie away from me.

We were only playing ball, only having a good time. I felt challenged, and I repeatedly slapped my hands against my thighs. "Charlie Farley! Gissit! Gis ya ball-y!"

Poor boy. He continued to look from me to her, his ball wedged firmly in his mouth. A flick of his tail showed me he was deciding who to go to—maybe because he was a sensitive soul who didn't want to hurt the feelings of the other, or, more than likely, he was contemplating who would keep throwing his ball for him. Delicately placing his prized toy on the ground, he nudged it so it rolled between us.

I was up for the challenge; I lurched to the side. Unfortunately, so did the 4X4 woman. Hands scrabbled to grab the red plastic ball, and it seemed more like a scrum at a rugby match than playtime with a canine pal. My hand secured the orb, only to be held fast in a strong grip. Sparks charged up my arm at the contact. Usually I would have dropped what I was holding, but no. My ball. Mine.

Tug. Heavy breathing. Another tug, a grinding of teeth. More heavy, laboured breathing, followed by an impatient woof from behind us.

With a surge of strength, I yanked the ball towards me, totally believing I would secure it. However, all I managed to do was tug the woman with it and be knocked flat by the complete weight of her body on top of mine, smacking my head on the ground in the process.

I opened my eyes and was momentarily struck dumb by the look of the woman now sprawled on top of me. Brown eyes were widened in shock, her mouth moving in apology. Seeing her so close up was totally breath taking, not to mention that the weight of her pressing on my chest made it ache.

"Yappp!"

Charlie was next to us, trying to poke his head between our stunned faces and get anyone's attention. We were each absorbed in trying to read the other's expression, and he was getting antsy.

"Ellie! What the fuck are you doing?" Abbie's voice came from the doorway.

I tried to squirm free, but I still didn't let go of the ball and neither would my rival.

"You fighting?" Abbie asked.

Dark hair whipped over my face as the woman turned to face my sister. I watched in rapt fascination as the stoic expression changed into a wonderful smile.

"Good afternoon. You two related?"

Nice start to the conversation, considering it came from an assailant who was pinning me to the floor. It was not the typical greeting someone would give in the middle of a wrestling match. And why wasn't Abbie kicking the woman's ass into 2013?

"She's my sister."

For fuck sake, Abbie! Get her off me! I felt the woman's laughter bubble up before it burst out into the air at my sister's comment.

"You've met Ellie, then?'

"Seems like we are getting to know each other."

I squirmed as if to remind her I was still pinned beneath her. Brown eyes turned my way, and she flashed me the most beautiful smile.

"Hi there, Ellie. Good to meet you."

Were her eyes twinkling? I gritted my teeth and was just about to give her a mouthful of unladylike epithets.

"Can I have my ball back?" the woman asked.

What was this? Some fucked up childhood re-enactment? Was I the evil old woman who lived next door, who wouldn't give a kid her ball back after it had crashed through my petunias?

"Your ball back?" Abbie moved into the room and stood next to us. "Hello there, little fella."

Charlie licked her hand and then turned his attention back to the scrappers.

"I think she means your ball back, don't you?" She ruffled the fur behind Charlie's ears before directing her attention to us again. "Would either of you like to tell me what is going on?"

I relaxed momentarily, and in doing so I released my vice-like grip on the ball.

My captor didn't waste any time. She manoeuvred the spherical object away in one fluid movement, then she was off me as if she had bounced off my body like it was a trampoline.

"Ooof!"

"Woof!"

Shaking her body, the woman turned to Abbie and stuck out her ball-free hand—the one that wasn't a thief—and announced, "Emily Carson. Carson Property Developments."

So, she had a name and a business. Who cared?

"Abigail Culligan." Looked as if my sister cared. "And this one trying to get up is my sister, Ellie McSmelly."

Emily Carson's face scrunched in thought as she processed the nickname my sister thought highly hilarious.

"Ellie Anderson, actually."

Did I always sound so fucked off and distant? Maybe I sounded like that because I had lost the ball and, along with it, the attention of the little brown-eyed boy. I felt a scratching sensation on my calf and noticed that Charlie was trying to get my attention. I ruffled the fur on the top of his head.

"Lovely to meet you, Abigail and...Ellie."

Did she deliberately hesitate over my name to annoy me even more?

"This is Charlie, the dog I am hoping to adopt."

"So, it's not final then?" Why was I being such a bitch? A totally hot woman was standing in front of me, the woman I had felt the need to see up close and personal, and I was being a total twat just because she was hoping to adopt the dog I had met moments ago. I needed to get a grip.

"Huh?"

"I said..." Maybe the grip I had been hoping to get wasn't quite ready to be gripped. "You haven't adopted Charlie yet? It's not final?"

"What do you mean by that? It's not final? I came here today to meet with him, and then you came and intruded on our time."

Anger flared up inside me. "Sorry. I didn't see the notice on the door." I marched over to the doorway, swung the door back and pretended to examine it. "Nope. Nothing there."

"Ellie!"

The concern in Abbie's voice should have served as a warning. I wasn't acting like myself. Maybe it was the effects of the vodka and Cokes from the previous night. As a matter of fact, I didn't feel well. My stomach was kicking off and doing a line dance to my throat. I knew it was a matter of moments before the remnants of anything I had eaten or drunk in the last few hours were on display to one and all.

"Ex-cuse...me." And I was gone, flying down the corridor in search of the nearest toilet. Thankfully my stomach waited until my mouth was situated within target range before it gave the big heave ho and treated me to a rendition of Psychedelic Pizza artwork with a backing track of gagging noises.

By the time I had thrown up, cried about throwing up, washed my face and rinsed out my mouth, I felt a little better. Embarrassed, but better. Why had I wrestled with Emily Carson? Why had I all but challenged her for the ownership of Charlie? Charlie was a dog in need of a good home, lots of love and attention, not two women fighting over his ball on the floor of his kennel. I should go and apologise for my actions, blame my stupidity on not feeling well before shaking Emily's hand and wishing her well with her life with the gorgeous Charlie. That's what people do when they are grown up.

Walking back into the room where I had last seen Abbie, Emily, and Charlie, I was greeted by silence. Where had everybody gone? I made my way back to where I had last seen Lily and Rob. No one was there, either. It suddenly struck me that it was actually rather quiet for a dog pound—no whimpers, no staff around. It was like a canine Marie Celeste.

Then I heard a squeal followed shortly by excited yaps. I followed the sounds down the corridor and exited through a doorway marked "Yard."

Not surprisingly, there stood Abbie, Rob, and Emily chatting away whilst Lily played with two dogs off the lead. One was the Jack Russell I had seen her trying to kiss through the bars, and the other was the main man himself, Charlie. Lily was throwing the red ball for the dogs to chase. Funny how Emily didn't have a problem with other people touching her balls… That hadn't sounded right.

Watching Charlie playing with the other dog and my niece, I felt that special glow again. Why was I so smitten with the little chap? There were plenty of dogs in need of a loving home, so why him? And why now? I hadn't intended to adopt a pooch when I had slipped into the back of the car earlier, so why was I contemplating fighting Emily Carson for Charlie?

At that precise moment, deep brown eyes spotted me. An excited yelp issued from his mouth, and he sprinted over to where I was standing, the ball forgotten.

I knelt down and cupped his head, then scratched behind his ears, which made him grin and pant. "You like that, buddy? Yeah...it's good, isn't it?"

As soon as I spoke, Charlie moved away, as if to go back to Emily, but then came back to me, before moving towards Emily again. It was totally a Skippy moment, and I wanted to say "Is Billy down the well, Skip?" Instead, I took the hint and followed him to where the adults were congregated. It was time to make nice.

Conjuring a friendly smile from the depths, I stuck out my hand. "Hello. My name is Ellie Anderson. Nice to meet you."

Emily hesitated, as if she was contemplating what might be a hidden agenda beneath the gesture.

Did she think I would pull her over and pin her to the ground? Actually, was I considering doing that?

"Seems like we got off on the wrong foot. Sorry about that. I have no idea why I behaved as I did." Part of that statement was true. I wasn't exactly sure why I had wrestled with the woman standing in front of me, except that I wanted to get the ball, thus keeping Charlie with me.

I watched in fascination as her sombre expression changed into something truly breath taking. Emily Carson had to be the most beautiful women I'd ever seen in all of my thirty- three years. Her hand slipped into mine, and I felt the shock again, the same shock I had experienced when her hand had covered mine in the fight for the ball. Instead of releasing our handshake, we held on a little bit longer than was customary.

"Erm...no worries. Nice to finally get to meet you."

Brown eyes met mine, and there was a question in their depths. Maybe she was also wondering about the spark that had passed between us, or even why I was still holding on to her hand.

At that thought, I pulled my hand away sharply and shoved it into my pocket. I willed myself to stop staring at Emily, but I couldn't seem to tear my eyes away. It wasn't just because she was beautiful, it was something else, but I couldn't put my finger on what that "something else" was.

A small cough from beside me snapped me out of my fascinated fixation on the stunning Emily. I turned my attention towards Abbie. "Something in your throat?"

She bit her lip and swallowed back a swear word before she shot a forced grin in my direction. "We were just telling Emily about your landscaping business."

I wanted to say "And?" but held it back. After all, I was trying to make an effort to be nice.

"She has just bought Miller's Farm House and wants to sort out the gardens."

Instead of being happy that my sister was trying to pimp my business, I felt a deep urge to throttle her. She was doing it again—trying to fix me up with any available woman she could find, even if the woman was straight.

"Yes. I need to make it safe for Charlie."

Talk about a double slap—my sister trying to fix me up with Emily, and Emily rubbing it in about her being Charlie's new mummy. Where did that leave me? Hankering after two things that would never be mine, that's where.

"Here's my card." As if by magic, a neat little business card with "Carson Property Developers" stamped across the centre was between the tips of my fingers.

"Oh...erm...right." I started to give her my card, but she held up her hand.

"No need. Your sister has already given me one."

Yes. I bet she has. And a rundown of my life to date, if I knew Abbie.

"I've heard of your business. All good."

I smiled and nodded, as I didn't trust myself to speak at that moment.

"I'd love it if you could come to my place and have a look at my grounds."

Was she bragging? Just because I had only one acre didn't

mean it wasn't prime land, plenty enough land to keep one pup very happy. "Sure." Another smile to seal the deal. "Let me know when."

"Tomorrow too soon?" Emily asked.

Shit. Yes. "Great. I'll see you there about one," I answered. *I'll call in the morning and cancel. Yep. My wonderful plan.*

"Could we make it a little later? Say three? I'm coming to see Charlie at twelve."

Go on. Rub it in. I nodded and turned to look at the chap in question.

He was seated next to Lily, lapping up all the attention she could give to two dogs at once. It was as if he knew I was looking at him, as he turned and wagged his tail before yapping just the once as if to say "What?" Bless his furry paws.

"Looks like he wants a walk." Emily stepped in front of me, blocking my view of Charlie. "Nice to meet you, Ellie. See you tomorrow." And she was gone, taking the lad I had fallen for with her.

Chapter Two

The car ride back to Abbie's was filled with Lily's excited chatter. They were adopting Poppy, the Jack Russell, although Lily wanted to call her Jessie J, something that would NOT be happening.

With the Dogs Trust it wasn't just a case of saying, "Yep. I want that one." You had to show you were capable of looking after a pet, and one of the main requirements was having a suitable home and garden.

I grinned. A safe garden. A garden the dog could have freedom in, but also not be able to escape from. Another grin. Emily Carson was looking to me to make her garden safe enough for a home visit, so she could give Charlie her home and not mine. For a fleeting moment, I felt a little more powerful.

Abbie, Rob, and Lily had to make a commitment to Poppy. They had to go to the Trust every day to bond with Poppy and to allow her to get to know them. Fortunately, their garden was safe, and their house was dog-proof. They were also very keen to adopt Poppy—another plus. I liked the way the Trust operated. They didn't allow just anyone to take a dog; the person had to be right, and the dog had to be happy. This rule applied to everyone. Everyone.

I grinned again.

"Do you like Poppy, Aunty Wellie?"

"She's an angel, Lil."

"No she ain't. She's a dog."

Kids. Gotta love 'em.

After dinner, Rob had a football game was calling his name, and he scuttled off to the living room, taking a sleepy Lily with him. She loved to curl up next to him on the sofa when he was watching TV, though I doubted she would get much sleep with all his shouting "Are you blind?" at the ref.

I helped Abbie clear away the pots and was the drier to her washing up. I knew she wanted to talk about something, and I knew what that "something" was going to be.

"Emily's nice, isn't she?"

I continued to dry.

"She has a good reputation as a developer."

I slipped another dry plate onto the stack.

"And she's gay."

Smash.

"Watch my plates, sis."

I knelt down and started to collect the pieces of what had so recently been one of Abbie's dinner plates. Without looking up, I asked, "And I suppose that just came up in conversation, did it?"

Abbie joined me on the floor, dustpan and brush in hand. "Not really, no. I observed many things that told me her preference leaned to the Sapphic side." She paused whilst she chased a stubborn sliver of china around on the tile. "Her key ring for one—Stonewall. The sticker in the back window of her car— Stonewall. The ring on her pinkie finger—"

"Was that Stonewall too?"

Abbie stood and smacked me on the back of the head. "Git. No."

I rubbed the spot as I stood too, but she moved to throw the pieces away.

"And the way she stared at you constantly when she thought you weren't looking."

My heart banged dramatically inside my chest, as if it was auditioning for a new play called Hope. "That means nothing, Abbie. People look at each other all the time."

Abbie laughed. "True. But not in the panting 'I want you' kind of way."

"Pfffft!"

"You can 'pfffft' all you want. It was totally obvious. Emily Carson wants you badly."

Green eyes met green, and I knew that Abbie wasn't pulling my leg. She might be indulging in a bout of wishful thinking, but at that precise moment, she believed every word that she was saying.

"I have to go. See you soon, okay?"

Abbie tilted her head and looked at me.

"Before you start matchmaking, remember that you promised me."

Abbie sighed and nodded.

"And I really have to go. It seems as if I have to go take a look at Miller's Farm tomorrow."

Before I left, I wished Rob a quiet goodbye, as Lily was snoring on the sofa next to him.

I had just opened the door to my pickup when Abbie came up behind me. Her hands slipped around my waist and turned me around to give me a hug. Her soft voice whispered in my ear, "I know how much it hurt today. And how much you still miss Toby. We all do, sis."

A pressure swelled inside my chest, and I nodded against her shoulder.

"One day, eh?"

A sniff, another nod, and a croaked, "Yes. One day."

When I arrived home, I went straight to the walk-in closet in my bedroom. On the shelf above the clothes rods were boxes full of memories—memories I wanted to forget, yet memories I wanted close to me. Boxes marked "Mum and Dad," boxes marked "Family," and a box marked "Toby."

I pulled the last box down and took it to the front room, where I settled myself on the beanbag and balanced the box on my thigh. When I lifted the lid, I was greeted by big brown eyes and a toothy grin, and my tears welled up. I lifted the picture closer and looked into my lad's eyes. If I tried hard enough, I could just make out my reflection in his pupils. I'd been younger, happier, and smitten right back. I carefully laid the picture to one side and selected another. This time Toby was nine months old, racing around the garden chasing a cat that had decided my back garden was the perfect place to sunbathe. Not on Toby's watch, it wasn't. A thick snorting laugh shot out of my mouth, followed by a sob.

Each picture was like the pleasure/pain theory. It hurt so much to see him, yet it soothed my soul to know that I had had someone so special to share my world with. Glossy prints of the best thirteen years of my life—every stage a reminder of what I'd had and what I had lost.

It had been five years since I had said my farewell to him, and five years since I had last looked at his picture. I felt guilty, almost like I had abandoned his memory, but it had hurt so much to look, hurt so much to remember.

Two hours later, I slipped all the photographs back into the box and closed the lid. Instead of putting it back on the shelf, I set it on the coffee table. It was time to move on…time to bring Toby out of the dark and me along with him. I would buy a photo album, buy some frames. I wanted to see him again. Time, as they say, was a great healer, and although the pain never truly goes away, it does get easier to deal with. My dad always said that pets were here to show us how to love, and although it seems cruel that they are taken from us too soon, their love carries on. Love is something we should treasure, not hide from. It was a pity that when it came to loving me, my dad couldn't measure up to his own words.

I had decided that I wasn't going to hide anymore. Tomorrow I would go and see Charlie again. I knew Emily wanted to be his mum, but I thought, maybe, I could be that too.

I guess it might have been a little underhanded for me to go to the Dogs Trust at nine o'clock the next morning when I knew

Emily was going at twelve. Who cared? Not me. As I had looked into Charlie's eyes, I'd felt something click into place, something I thought I would never feel again. If it turned out that the Trust decided Emily was the better parent, then so be it. I would take the rejection well. Maybe.

A woman greeted me at the door, and then her face showed confusion as I asked to see Charlie.

"Charlie has someone interested in adopting him." Her voice quavered. "Just let me…" She toddled off to the reception desk and tapped a password into the computer which brought the screen to life.

"Are you Emily Carson?"

She knew I wasn't Emily, but was politely informing me that the adoption of Charlie was underway. Why else have it all on the system?

Turning, she gave me the traditional "I'm sorry" face before attempting to actually say the words.

It was time to turn on what little charm I possessed, and that wasn't a lot. "I just want to see him. He is so adorable, isn't he?"

The woman smiled and nodded. "That's the problem. They all are."

I surreptitiously glanced at her name badge before smiling widely. "People like you, Ann, amaze me."

Her smile wavered. "People like me?" She paused momentarily before continuing. "Why would someone like me amaze anyone?"

"Because if it wasn't for people like you, where would our canine friends be? Who would look out for them?"

Ann laughed. Loudly. "Nice try."

I scrunched up my face showing her I knew I'd been caught, which made her laugh again, and this time I joined her. After a moment, we fell silent, Ann's eyes looking at me expectantly.

"I know someone else wants to adopt him, but when I saw him yesterday, I didn't get the chance to speak to anyone about adopting him myself."

Ann looked deeply into my eyes as if exacting a promise of sorts from me, then she sighed and nodded. "Come on then. Let's make Charlie's day."

As she moved past me, I wanted to pump the air with my fist and hiss "yes!" but decided that, for the moment, I should at least give the appearance of being mature enough to adopt a dog.

As we walked through to the back, the mischievous side of me wanted to drop hints about seeing Emily yesterday and how she didn't seem to connect with the pooch. But, nah...that wasn't my style. Everything had to be fair and square.

Who was I kidding? It had nothing to do with being fair and square. I couldn't do that to Emily. God help me, I liked her. Was attracted to her. I mean, how many women had I known that had made me react the way I had reacted to her? I'd never felt an actual spark when touching someone. Never before needed to look at the colour of someone's eyes so badly. And seeing her with Charlie... I sighed. I felt guilty about being at the kennel, but I also wanted to see the little man again. Just the once. Just to see if the connection I had with him was the same today as yesterday.

Approaching his kennel, the same excitement welled up in me. I'd brought my own ball for him to chase, bought first thing that morning from the pet store. To say Charlie was happy to see me would have been an understatement. He was dozing in his basket when I arrived, his back to the bars, but he lifted his head and sniffed the air inquisitively. He turned, got up, and came to me, all in one fluid movement.

"Hey, baby."

"Yap!" He was on his hind legs, his tail flapping wildly.

"Want to play?"

Charlie tilted his head back and made a mini howling noise, his paws scrabbling at the cage.

Ann laughed. "It seems as if it will be okay to leave you two on your own. You can play in the yard."

Playing ball is such a simple thing. All you need is a ball and willing participants. It can last for as little or as long as you want—your call. Some people might think that throwing a ball, having it brought back, and then throwing it again is a waste of time. Those same people think that half an hour could be better spent, even if it is used for sorting out the niggling things that life can throw at you. Not me. Half an hour throwing the ball for Charlie was the best possible use of my time. Watching him chase it, pin it, growl at it as he pretended it was his prisoner, then trot back grinning for me to throw it again—that, to me, was fulfilling. Seeing him nudge it with his nose when I pretended I didn't see it; hearing his impatient yap; being jumped on and thoroughly licked with happiness—definitely not a waste of time. And in this short thirty minutes, I knew, without the shadow of a doubt, I was in love.

Saying goodbye to him was hard, but I had to go, as Emily would be arriving in just over an hour and a half. I wanted to speak to the volunteers about his adoption, wanted to find out why his owners had given up on such a gem as Charlie. I left him with a squeaky toy and a promise to visit him the next day.

After speaking to Sharon, Charlie's key worker, about why he was at the Trust, I realised that some people should be shot. I couldn't help the tears that came when I found out about the neglect, the beatings, the abandonment Charlie had suffered at the hands of someone who probably classed him or herself as being superior to a dog.

Charlie had been found at the beginning of October the previous year, scavenging through bins. He was painfully underweight, had injuries to his hind leg, and open wounds around his neck, probably caused by being tethered. Injuries of that extent should have made him wary of humans, should have made him fearful of trusting another person, but no. When the call came through from a concerned party about a dog looking like it needed help, members of the Trust had gone to save him. Instead of running or cowering, Charlie had wagged his tail and limped over to them, curling himself into a ball around Sharon's feet. It was if he knew they were there to help him.

He had needed immediate medical attention. Surgery on his hind leg treated a fracture and a ruptured cruciate; eighteen stitches were needed near his right ear, twenty-eight around his neck. They also found a wound at the back of his neck that suggested the owner had cut out the microchip that identified him with his owner. At that juncture, I wanted to use a very bad word that started with a C.

Charlie's adoption had been on hold until he was healed and feeling more secure about the world around him. Even though people could meet him now, it would be another month before he would be ready to go home with his new mummy because of all he had been through.

Sharon gave me a form to fill out, once again making sure I knew that someone else was interested in Charlie.

The image of Emily's smiling face flitted into my mind, and I felt guilty all over again. It didn't stop me from filling in the form, didn't stop me from taking one of their small photographs of Charlie and slipping it inside my purse.

All day, I thought of Charlie. Thought of the way he trusted, the way his tail wagged, the way he loved humans. How could that be? How could a dog who had so obviously been mistreated open himself up for anything? Countless times I slipped his photograph from my purse and stared at his sparkling eyes, his grinning mouth, and read the text at the side that introduced Charlie to the world as "Loveable, friendly, playful."

At three o'clock, I pulled into the driveway of Miller's Farm. Seeing Emily dressed in cargo pants and a sweatshirt made my heart flip flop inside my chest. She was halfway up a ladder, sanding the window sill of one of the upstairs windows with an electric sander, her ears covered with sound reducing muffs. As she stretched, her sweatshirt lifted and exposed a very muscled back. I could tell she was strong by the way she manoeuvred herself, making the sander do her bidding.

She was so beautiful, so captivating, so positively breath taking. Yet she was going to take Charlie away from me. Or I was going to take him from her. Guilt flooded through me. Here I was, her potential employee, stabbing her in the back when she wasn't looking. Why was I doing that? Why was I contemplating sneaking something away from her when she, in fact, had seen Charlie first?

I reached for my purse and then pulled out the picture again. God. That face. Those eyes. My grin spread like butter, and I nodded at the picture.

BANG BANG BANG! Fuck!

"When were you going to tell me you were planning on trying to steal *my* dog?"

What the fuck? The surprise of seeing Emily standing next to the car window nearly made me pee my pants.

"Sneaking over to the Trust. I know. They fucking told me."

I was glad my doors were locked. Judging by the look on her face, I could have been the next victim of her electric sander.

"Charlie is not YOUR dog."

She gritted her teeth, tipped her head to the side, and clutched the sander more firmly, as if she wanted to batter me about the head with it.

"By the way, your mobile doesn't work."

Huh? Why bring that up now?

"So I'll tell you to your face—get the fuck off my land and stay away from my dog."

And there's the answer.

As an aside, I couldn't help noticing that Emily Carson looked magnificent when she was angry. My smile sneaked up from nowhere. I didn't do it to piss her off; it just reflected how I was feeling. Even when Emily was threatening me, hating me, it felt good being with her.

"Go on. Look fucking smug. But I'm telling you now, Charlie is my dog."

"But I—"

"But you nothing. Go!"

Instead of me going, she did. She spun on her heel and marched inside her house, leaving me staring after her.

I had two choices. One, go. Two, go after her. I chose the latter.

I didn't knock, didn't announce I was there; I just went inside and looked for her. She was easy to find, as she was in what was going to be her living room, her hands resting on the mantelpiece, her head bowed. Even before I reached her, I knew she was crying. Those strong shoulders were shaking, and soft noises were escaping from the shroud of her hair.

I gently laid my hand on her back and braced myself for a

bollocking, but it didn't come.

Emily turned and wrapped her arms around me, her sobs settling onto my shoulder.

I felt so protective of her, like I could stop her crying and somehow make her feel better. The only thing I could think of to accomplish that was to promise I wouldn't see Charlie again. I wanted to—God, I wanted to promise her that—but I couldn't. So, I continued to hold her, stroking my hand up and down her back, comforting her with shushing sounds and small kisses sporadically placed on the top of her head. Her fingers dug into my back, holding me until her crying eased.

"I'm sorry. I...don't usually get angry." A loud hiccough made her chest heave. "Or cry like this."

I remained silent. When Emily pulled away, I saw the utter anguish in her face. Her eyes were puffy and her cheeks were streaked, as the tears had made tracks through what I imagined was paint dust on her skin.

"Why, Ellie?" Brown eyes searched my own, seeking an answer. "Why did you do it?"

I shrugged and pulled away from her. I felt embarrassed, and not just about my actions. If Emily and I were ever going to salvage anything—be it friendship, a working relationship, or something more special—I had to explain.

With my face turned away from her, I found the strength to start my story. "His name was Toby. A Border Terrier. He was my best friend at a time when I really needed one." I walked over to the other side of the room and pretended to be interested in an old table, running my fingers over the distressed wood. "When I first got him, I was fifteen years old. I'd wanted a dog for years, but my parents had always said no."

I spilled each and every detail about my connection to Toby—

why he was so damned important to me, so bloody special. "He stood by me when others didn't, showed me that no matter who I chose to love, he still loved me exactly the same." I turned my head so I could see her.

Emily was still in the same spot I had left her, her expression unreadable.

I let out a huge breath. "When I was twenty, I came out. I told my parents I was gay, and I expected we would move on from there. Abbie didn't care; I was still Ellie. My parents..." I clicked my tongue, "...weren't so understanding."

"Oh, Ellie, I'm so sorry."

I shrugged. The time for ruing the lack of parental acceptance was well past its "sell by" date. "I haven't spoken to them in nearly thirteen years." This wasn't about them, though. This was about the "why," although maybe they were at least a part of the reason. I didn't know for sure.

I no longer cared as much about the rejection from my parents. Too much had happened in my life since then for me to fret over their insensitivity and inability to love me no matter what. Unlike Toby.

"Abbie and Rob took me in. Gave Toby and me a home. Got me on my feet again. I lost Toby to cancer five years ago. I had to have him euthanised. It was the hardest decision I've ever had to make."

I was finding it difficult to talk. My throat seemed to have swollen, and words were becoming trapped. I begged myself not to start crying, not in front of Emily. It seemed, of late, the waterworks turned on easily, and I couldn't seem to completely shut off the flow. 2012 was turning into the year of crying. It seemed as if that was all I had done since yesterday.

Emily moved closer to me, her face full of concern. Her hand reached towards mine, but stopped.

It didn't take a genius to work out why I had fallen so hard for Charlie, although I knew he was not Toby, and he would never replace my lad. Charlie would always be Charlie, and even if he did look his predecessor, there were many differences between them. For a start, Toby never liked red balls. At that thought, I snorted, a laugh that immediately turned into a sob. It was so hard to hold in the emotion. At that moment, undoubtedly people who had never had a pet would have been wondering what all the fuss was about.

Emily's arms slipped around me, and it was her turn to be the comforter.

Being held by Emily was something I knew I would never tire of. It seemed as if I slotted right into the circle of her protection and, as long as I was there, nothing and no one could hurt me.

She let me cry. When the tears finally turned into gasping, she led me to the kitchen and plonked me down on one of the dining chairs. When Emily moved away from me, I immediately felt the loss of our contact. The sound of a kettle being filled, the click of the switch, and she was back, pulling a chair close to me.

I lifted my head and looked deeply into her eyes. It wasn't pity I saw there, but understanding.

Her hand stretched out and she caught my fingers with hers, her thumb stroking the back of my thumb. She was thinking something over. I could tell by the way she nibbled her bottom lip, the way her eyebrows dipped.

"Look." She straightened, but didn't release her hold on my hand. "We can both see Charlie."

I didn't understand.

"They always say that it isn't a person who chooses a dog, but the other way around."

I still didn't get it. Call me thick—I do on a regular basis.

"After the month is up, we will see who Charlie has bonded with most closely, okay?"

What? "I don't understand."

A delightful giggle came from her mouth. "We will let Charlie decide who he wants to live with. But," she leaned closer, "we will see him together. No sneaking off to get extra time with him, okay?"

I nodded. At least it was a start. It might turn out that after a month, I was still no better off, but at least I would be friends with the person that loved the same dog I did. It seemed like a plan.

Chapter Three

Two hours later I pulled up outside my house. I'd looked over the work Emily wanted done, and it wasn't as extensive as I first believed. I should have it completed by the time D-Day arrived. Her house still needed some renovation, but most of the larger jobs were already done—new central heating and windows, roofing tiles replaced, plumbing working. The landscaping would be a case of cosmetic surgery. She would be working inside, while I was working out. And because I was spending time at her place, it would be easier for us to visit the Dogs Trust. Together. That made me smile.

I couldn't start the work immediately, I was committed to finishing a couple of other jobs I already had lined up, but they should be completed by the Friday. I did have some other people who were waiting, but I organised a couple of blokes I used on occasion to start them for me. All in all, it would all work out as planned. By Friday night, I would be all hers.

Sleep was a weird bugger. It was elusive, yet when I did catch the proverbial forty winks, my dreams were vivid. I would like to be able to say they were full of me and Emily having a wonderful time—maybe walking Charlie or seated in a restaurant chatting and laughing. But no. They were the horrible kind, the ones that make you wake up in a sweat and thank God they weren't real just before you questioned if they were actually dreams. Images from years past filtered into my mind—the look of hatred from my mother, the disappointment from my father, leaving my home and hearing their scornful yells following me. Not good. I can still remember the look Toby gave me as we bundled ourselves into my car and drove away. It was gently questioning. The same look he had given me at the vet's.

Enough. I couldn't take the dreams anymore. All I wanted was to put that chapter of my life behind me and move on. So, I got up, dressed, and went to work earlier than usual.

Luckily, the work I was finishing off was for two new homes that had just been built, so I wasn't disturbing anyone. I spent the morning planting Hebe, primarily H. Andersonii, H. Ellie, and H. Mauve Queen. Ellie and Andersonii—I couldn't help it if they named the plants after me, could I? But I had to admit, I was definitely NOT the Queen of Mauve.

Before I knew it, it was noon, time to go and pick up Emily. If we went together, we could be sure we would arrive at the kennels at the same time. It wasn't that we had trust issues, though maybe we were each still a little wary of the other. I had learned my lesson the day before; there was no way I wanted to see Emily cry again.

The feeling of excitement started long before I pulled into her road. It was a pleasant fluttering in my stomach. Initially I put it down to going to see Charlie, but I would have been lying if

I'd said that was the only reason. When I spotted Emily waiting for me at the end of her driveway, the sensation jumped from my stomach and into my throat. It made me feel like jumping up and down with joy.

When Emily caught my eye, she gave me that gorgeous grin. God, she was beautiful—the wind making her hair dance, those alluring brown eyes, that smile... Jesus. I didn't know if my poor heart could take it.

"Hey, you. You're early."

"And yet you're waiting."

She thought about it a moment, and then her laughter floated in the air like music. "True."

Soon she was seated next to me, and I slapped the pickup into gear and began our drive to see the main man.

Sharon greeted us both, her face saying everything her mouth didn't. I don't think she expected to see Emily and me at the same time, considering we were both wanting to adopt the same dog. Charlie was waiting for us, his lead hanging from his mouth and a manic tail wagging in greeting. We decided to walk him in the woods, as the weather was dry and we wouldn't end up looking like beasts from the swamp by the time we got back. It was weird. We both wanted to hold his lead, but we each kept trying to pass it over to the other. Finally we stopped arsing about and decided to take turns. How civilised we were becoming.

It seemed like Charlie knew he was the focus and loved every minute of it. As I clicked his lead to his collar, I noticed the irregular growth of the hairs on his neck. I pushed the fur aside and could see the scars where his wound had healed. Amazingly, he let me do it, let me examine the evidence of the cruelty he had been subjected to.

"Poor baby. I wish I knew who had done this to him."

Emily didn't answer. Thinking she hadn't heard me, I turned to repeat it. Her face was contorted with anger, and she just shook her head and looked away. I knew she needed to walk him so she could lavish love on him, bathe him in the goodness that can come far more easily than hatred.

"Here. You take him first," I said.

The weather was nippy, but the walk was wonderful all the same. Charlie was interested in everything—every tree, each blade of grass, and a squirrel. I have to admit, I felt sorry for the squirrel at one point. The sound of Charlie whining and yelping must've frightened the crap out of it. And me, too, as he always waited until I was submerged in my own world of thought before he kicked off.

Twenty-five minutes into the walk, Emily held the lead out to me. "Your turn."

The smile she bestowed on me was blinding, and I felt like a teenager. Reaching for the lead, I once again felt the spark race from her to me. Why was this happening? Was there something wrong with me? Had my time with power tools made me electric? Or her, for that matter. She did use power tools more than I did, after all.

"Did you feel that?" Her voice was almost a whisper, almost reverent. "Every time you touch my hand, it's as if a spark shoots through me."

A blush rose along my neck. I couldn't understand why I was embarrassed. It wasn't as if I had anything to do with the fact that we interacted with one another like eels just about to fight.

"Erm." Nice save, Anderson. Three letter word. Good job I wasn't playing Scrabble. "Yes." Come on! More! "I did feel it." Fantastic. Bravo. And the award for the most inspiring speech goes to...

And that was it. I grinned inanely, showing my teeth like a village idiot, and walked away in the way people do when they are pretending they are being pulled by their dog.

Back at the centre, I unclipped Charlie's lead and let him run around the yard for a while before taking him back to his kennel. I felt badly about leaving him there, but he seemed happy enough to climb into his basket and chew on his Woofer. Honestly. That's what they're called. And if you want to know what's in them—think of a bull's— Nah... I can't say it. Every time I think of it, my stomach roils and I feel the need to brush my teeth, use mouthwash, shower, and then do it all again. We promised Charlie that we would return the next day, and then we left.

The drive back to Emily's was quiet, as we were each in our own little world. It wasn't uncomfortable, far from it. It was as if we had done this a thousand times and were used to the contented silence.

As I pulled up outside her house, I wanted to say something magnificent, something profound and lasting. "See you tomorrow. Same time." Wow. I outdid myself on that one. I guessed she wouldn't sleep a wink that night, trying to work out the message hidden behind my carefully chosen words.

The afternoon stint at work lasted longer than I'd anticipated, and considering I'd been up and about earlier than the crack of Hades, I was well and truly spent. I got home at gone seven and was knackered.

My answer phone was blinking rapidly, as if it had something in its eye. Lame, but hey... I was tired, okay? Three messages. Not bad. Only three. The first was from my sister, asking if it was really me she'd seen pulling out of the Dogs Trust car park with the gorgeous, dark haired property developer.

Crap.

The second message was from the gorgeous property developer herself, asking if we could go to see Charlie earlier the next day, as she had to pick up supplies from the DIY centre.

Sure. No problem.

Third message was my sister again, squealing, "It was you. I knew it. Will you be seeing her again?"

What the fuck? How did she know?

Abbie answered my call on the second ring. She was out of breath, which was surprising, considering she always had her mobile on some part of her anatomy.

Her usual hello was replaced by a torrent of questions, all fired at bullet speed, and all of them concerning my appearance at the Dogs Trust with Emily. I cocked my head to the side, pulled the phone away from my ear, and let her ramble.

When I heard the receiver go quiet, I put it back to my ear. "Hey, sis. How're you?'"

"Cut it and spill."

"Is that a medical procedure?" I waited for a smart retort that didn't come. "Cut what exactly?"

Abbie went quiet for a millisecond and then spoke with exaggerated slowness, as if she had suddenly become convinced that I was, in fact, as stupid as she thought I was. "So—are—you—seeing—Emily—as—a—poten-tial girlfriend?"

I tutted, as if I had suddenly become convinced idiocy ran in the family. "Why is that when you see me with a woman, you automatically assume I want to cop off with her?"

"No I don't. Because you are never with a woman. That's the problem."

"We both want to adopt Charlie—you know, the Border." Sparkling brown eyes danced in front of my face, and I realised they weren't Charlie's but Emily's as I dropped her off. I coughed and straightened up. "So, we decided to both visit him at the same time and see who he prefers."

"R-iiig-hhht."

That was the word she always used that way when she didn't believe a word I was saying. I wasn't about to defend myself; I had nothing to defend. I was telling the truth as I knew it.

"And it wouldn't hurt for you to get better acquainted with Ms Carson in the process, would it?"

I heard a snigger and knew my brother-in-law was listening to our conversation. I could imagine Abbie pulling faces and mouthing words at him.

"The relationship between Emily and me is purely business." Even as I said it, I didn't believe it myself. No wonder Abbie started laughing. "I haven't got time for this, Abs. You promised you wouldn't stir the shit. Bye."

I heard her mutter "But she—" before I clicked "end call."

"But she" what? God! Sometimes my sister did my head in. Actually, more often than not, I did my own head in. Why did I care what Emily thought or said? The only thing between us was Charlie, and to me, he was the most important thing of all.

Thirty minutes later, I was showered and heating up soup, as I couldn't be arsed cooking anything proper to eat. I wanted to get to bed and try and catch up on missed sleep. It wasn't until I was halfway through my evening "meal" that I remembered I hadn't called Emily back. Part of me was excited about hearing her voice again, but the more sensible and impossible side decided to text her instead. Until I remembered my buggered up mobile phone. I'd been so busy trying to undercut Emily on seeing Charlie, I'd forgotten to get a new phone. I would've tried to fix the old one, but thinking about putting my phone next to my face after it had swum about in the bog at the nightclub... Nah. It had to be a new one or risk an SDI to the face.

It took me an hour to pluck up the courage to call her back. Stupid, I know. It was only a "That's fine. I'll pick you up at eleven." So why was I being all Joan Crawford? I really missed my trusty piss-soaked mobile phone. I can't tell you how many times I picked up her business card and put it back on the table, how many times I pressed all but one of the digits and then cut it off.

"Come on, you chicken shit. Call her."

I was pissing myself off now. A phone call. One. I wasn't calling the Prime Minister on Question Time on a live show; it was just Emily.

"Right. That is it, Anderson." Grabbing the phone I gritted my teeth. My hand slapped the business card on the table, and I dragged it over to me as if I was nabbing a criminal who was trying to escape. I don't know why I muttered, "You're my bitch, now." Maybe because I had seen too many action films.

Before I could press even one number, the phone rang in my hand. Staring stupidly at the thin black handset, I momentarily forgot what to do with it. It was as if my brain had farted and deleted my memory of how to press the green button for a nano-second.

"Erm...hello?" Not the telesales voice I had wanted, but at least I had been able to function—eventually.

"Erm...hello. Ellie?"

Shit. Shit. Crap and shit.

"This is Emily Carson here."

I know. I know. Fuck, I know.

"I just wondered if you got my message."

"Erm." Was I really a retard? "Message?" Yes. I was. "Oh,

your message. About tomorrow. Erm...yes. Yes. Erm...yes, that's fine." I think the yeses made it clear that the new time was okay. "Eleven, yes?"

I heard her release a breath and wondered whether she had been as nervous as I'd been. Nah. She was the gorgeous Emily Carson. She didn't do nervous.

"Great. I'll see you then." She paused. "And Ellie..."

"Yes?" Another yes. Was I sycophantic?

"Thanks for today. I had a great time with...with Charlie."

She was gone even before I had the chance to respond. Was it me, or had she paused before she said "Charlie"? Was she going to say something else, like she had a great time with me? Nah. No way. How could she have had a great time with me? I was just...me—not very special, not very special at all.

Being on the phone with Emily had been terrifying yet wonderful, almost like when you fancy someone but are too scared to say anything to them, but just love being the focus of their attention, even for a little while.

The "not very special" thing would not let go, and once again, I had a very disturbed night's sleep. At this rate, I would have circles under my eyes to rival those of Chi Chi the panda. No wonder pandas were on the verge of extinction if my face was any indication.

Chapter Four

T he next day started pretty much the same as the previous day, except for the voice of my sister inside my head trilling, "It wouldn't hurt for you to get better acquainted with Ms Carson in the process, would it?" I would have liked to say "no, it wouldn't", but I didn't want to take any chances, didn't want to put myself out there and risk a rebuff. Anyway, it was true what I'd said to Abbie. The relationship between Emily and me was purely to do with Charlie. It had taken me five years to even consider letting another inside my heart again, and there was no room for anything else—especially not my rival.

We took Charlie for another walk, which had to be no longer than forty-five minutes because his leg was still mending. Conversation was light between us, mainly sticking to things that were non-committal or impersonal. The weather—us Brits can talk about the weather for hours and never get bored, the up and coming Olympics, even the Queen's Diamond Jubilee were subjects of our ramblings. Of course there were times when I wanted to ask her more about herself, but a small part of me was scared I would become too interested in her. I know. I'm weird.

Charlie was full of beans and treated us both to his licks and his excitement. Watching him with Emily made me long for something more than what I had. The concept was elusive, but the feeling was strangely profound. It seemed so right to be walking through the woods on a cold January day with a beautiful woman and a gorgeous dog. The sound of our feet crunching through the leaves was comforting, almost familiar.

We played a while with Charlie upon our return, throwing the ball and watching him skitter all over the yard trying to fetch it and bring it back. It was funny to see him trying to decide who to give it to, but he was very much the gentleman and made sure we both got our turns.

This time, it was harder to leave him. It hurt more to put him back in his kennel and say, "See you tomorrow, little chap." But it had to be done.

When I pulled up outside Emily's house, I expected her to jump out and race off to the DIY centre, but she just stood there looking uncomfortable. Was she trying to come up with some way to tell me she didn't think our arrangement was working? That she'd thought it through and she wanted Charlie all to herself? A sinking feeling hit my gut. She wouldn't, would she?

"I was... I was thinking."

Yes, she was. She was going to freeze me out and take the furry lad for her own. A wave of adrenaline rushed through me and I was on the verge of telling her to shove it, when she finally continued.

"Have you had lunch?"

Had I had lunch?

"I, erm, have lunch here."

Good for you.

"And was wondering if you would like to, erm, share it."

Share her lunch? Why? I had a perfectly good lunch waiting for me back at work, so why would I want—

Clink. That was the sound of the penny dropping from a great height. It's a pity it didn't thwack me on the head as it passed.

"Never mind. I know how busy you are."

"No!" My explosive response was rather loud and eager sounding, but that was okay with me.

She nodded, and I detected some sort of dejection in the movement.

"No!" Okay. It was fine the first time, but now she was thinking her "lunch" idea was a no go. "I mean, yes!" Back to being a yes woman. "I mean— Aw, fuck it. I'd love to."

Finally! A response! There was hope for morons like me, after all, especially as I was rewarded with the most beautiful smile I'd ever seen. "I forgot my lunch this morning, so that would be wonderful." Why did I have to say that? She didn't want my fucking life story, even if it was a made up one.

"Great."

That smile again, sending a wonderful sensation rippling through my chest.

"I'll let you get parked while I get started on lunch." She turned away from me as if she was moving in slow motion. Strands of her hair separated and fluttered romantically around her head, and when she turned back, the smile replayed itself in slow motion, making her face even more stunning. "See you in a minute."

And then she was gone, leaving me mesmerised and immobile, my fingers aching to reach out and touch her, but too stunned to move.

It wasn't until I was seated at her dining room table that I remembered she'd said she wanted to go to the DIY centre. Was I keeping her back? Had she asked me to lunch out of politeness? I watched her making our sandwiches with grace and precision, and it didn't look as if she was eager to dash off anytime soon. For once my mouth decided not to drop me, or her, in it. I guiltily held on to the time I had with her.

Flash. A lightbulb. A huge, fuck off, lightbulb shot off in my noggin. I must've looked like a Sim with one of those green plumbobs above my head. Was she working me? Was I the Sim directed by her commands? Were my actions the result of a mere click of the mouse, and I was doing what she asked of me? Or was I going all RADA on my own ass? It was one of two things. She was either buttering me up to lay the bombshell about Charlie on me or...or...she actually wanted me to be there with her eating tuna salad sandwiches.

"Here you go." She slipped a plate in front of me, and then a cold glass of juice.

I looked up into warm brown eyes and felt the breath wheeze from me, and I knew my answer.

"I hope you like granary bread." Her musical laugh chimed. "Considering we have spent all morning together, I don't really know much about you."

And I really didn't know much about her, except that she was a property developer and she wanted my dog.

"Any dressing?"

I shook my head. When I opened my mouth, nothing came out. So I shook my head again and blushed furiously. For something to do, I took too large a bite of the sandwich and nearly choked. A strong hand slapped me on the back, and the errant piece of bread shot out of my mouth and landed ungraciously on the table. Social faux pas? You bet. Especially when I continued to cough and point lamely at my mouth.

More whacks and more coughing, followed by tears streaming down my face. I lifted my juice and spluttered some down, feeling the sting of it at the back of my throat. Emily looked at me with concern, her arm raised to hit me again.

"No...than-kk—yo—who."

Jesus. I couldn't even eat a sandwich when she was about. Another gulp of the cooling juice, and I felt a semblance of control over my vocal cords once again. But just to be on the safe side, I didn't risk speaking.

"You sure you're okay?"

I nodded and then took another sip.

She looked at me as if she was trying to work out whether I was lying. Apparently satisfied I wasn't about to keel over in my plate, she slipped into the seat next to me.

A few moments passed before I took another bite, this time smaller.

She waited until I had chewed and swallowed before she asked, "Everything okay?"

Raising the sandwich, I grinned. "Well, it hasn't killed me yet." Not really the wittiest thing I've ever said, but at least she laughed.

Ten minutes later, lunch was out of the way and it was back to me and her. As we'd been eating, I had thought of so many questions I wanted to ask her. Funnily enough, not one had involved Charlie.

"Coffee?"

"How old are you?" What the...

"Why? Has caffeine an age restriction?" Emily tilted her head and looked deeply into my eyes before saying, "I have decaf, if you're under the age limit."

"Sorry. I...I don't know where that came from."

"Yes you do. It is called human nature. That's what people do—ask questions."

Duh. I know that. But why blurt out a question you are not supposed to ask a lady? Had I pissed her off?

"I'm thirty-six, single, an only child, developed my own business from the money left to me by my parents, am very ambitious, and like to get what I want."

She didn't act as if I'd stepped over the boundaries of social etiquette for speaking to a woman. Actually, she looked beautiful. Her expression was open and honest, and her brown eyes sparkled.

My mouth went dry, very dry. She seemed to be expecting a response, but I didn't know what to say. I considered asking if the Stonewall collection she sported accurately reflected her sexual preference. She missed that out in her mini autobiography. Instead I asked, and I think you'll agree it was very radical of me, "So, erm, what do you want?"

Emily leaned forward until her face was only inches from mine. I could feel her breath on my face, and I inched closer to her. Dark eyes flickered down to my mouth and back to my eyes. One eyebrow rose up, and I watched her tongue slowly sweep across her lips.

"Well..."

The lump in my throat was larger than the chunk of sandwich had been. I didn't dare breathe, lest I cough in her face.

"One thing comes to mind."

Fuck. She was going to kiss me. She was going to kiss me.

And if you missed it, she was going to kiss me.

"I want you to tell me if you would like..."

Yes. I didn't care if I was being sycophantic. I wanted her to kiss me. A kiss was an unwritten promise.

"...a coffee."

Coffee? *A coffee?* Did kisses come in coffee cups? And why was I suddenly wanting her to kiss me? Where had the "there is no room for anything else" scenario I'd concocted earlier? She laughed and moved away, and I was left opened mouthed and feeling cheated.

I didn't want her to see how much she had affected me, so I leaned back on the chair and said, "Tea would be great. Milk, no sugar."

They do say pride goeth before a fall, and I was definitely feeling smugly proud of myself at that moment. Until the "fall" bit, as my chair tipped me backwards and flat on my arse. It wouldn't have been so embarrassing if I'd hadn't kicked the table on the way down and tipped that over with me. At least the smashing of plates covered my swearing.

I didn't have time to consider my fall from grace, as Emily was kneeling next to me, her face full of concern rather than laughter. "You okay?"

I nodded. I didn't trust my mouth to not spew out filth.

A slender hand stretched out to me, the fingers looking like those of a pianist rather than those of someone who was handy with power tools. "Here."

Hesitant, I reached out and clasped her hand. Even though it seemed to happen each time we touched, I was still surprised to feel the jolt that raced through me.

"There it is again." Emily's eyes sparked just as much as the shock of electricity.

My lips quivered until they decided to slip into a grin. "Must be my magnetic personality."

She cocked her head to the side, as she tended to do when she wanted to really look at something, and then that crooked grin slid into place.

My heart fluttered and bounced against my ribcage—something I used to believe would kill a person instead of making them feel more alive than they had in years.

In one pull she had me on my feet. I wanted to pretend to fall forward and into her arms, but it would have been a little obvious. Instead, I looked sheepish and stuffed my hands in my pockets.

"Erm... I'd better go." Her face displayed a fleeting look of disappointment, and I wanted to say I'd stay.

"I thought you wanted a cup of tea. Milk, no sugar."

"Sorry. Work beckons." In fact, I did need to go. Not because I had a million and one things to do, but because I didn't want anything to happen between me and Emily. I know, I'm up and down like a prostitute's underwear about how I wanted our relationship to pan out. If I did allow myself to become even a little bit interested—too late, was the cry—where would that leave me when it came to Charlie? If I crossed the boundary into acquaintance, or even friend, would that jeopardise how I would act when it came to who would get Charlie?

"You have to go to the DIY store anyway, so..."

"DIY store?" She looked confused, then it was as if she had transferred the plumbobs over to her own head and the light obviously clicked on. "Oh God! Yes! The DIY store."

I didn't say a word. It was apparent she had never intended to go to the DIY store and had completely forgotten all about having said it. I decided to call her on it. "I could give you a lift there if you want. I need to get more plant pots from the gardening section."

A look of mortification passed over her face, and she shook her head.

"It's no bother."

"I couldn't. Honestly. I've taken up so much of your—"

"I insist. You gave me lunch, it's the least I can do."

She gritted her teeth, then nodded resignedly.

"Meet you outside in a few." Before she could change her mind, I went to wait in the car. I have to admit, I laughed all the while.

Considering that her phone message had indicated it was imperative she get to the store, a bag of galvanised nails didn't seem like appointment-changing stuff.

I glanced at the small package and pulled the face that usually accompanies "Is that it?" but said nothing.

As I pulled into her driveway, I heard her unbuckling her seatbelt before the car stopped. My, she was in a rush to hide her shame.

"Thanks for that, Ellie. I...erm...they didn't have my order ready. I should've called to check."

Yeah, right.

"Same time tomorrow?"

I gave her a grin and nodded.

Emily scuttled off into the sanctuary of her home. Even so, I could have sworn I saw her watching me from the living room window as I pulled away.

A feeling of happiness washed over me. It had been a long

time since I had cared enough to look back in my rear view mirror to have a last look at a gorgeous woman. And before you say it, looking doesn't mean anything, okay?

I arrived home to find eleven messages on my answering machine, most of them from potential clients. I couldn't afford to miss jobs like that, and I didn't care to have my sister calling me as soon as I walked in the door to accuse me of changing the kennel time because she had seen me with Emily the previous day.

"What did you think I'd do? Marry you off?" was the first thing she said as I answered the phone, and the rest of the conversation wasn't much better.

The next morning, I went and bought a mobile phone before I did anything else. The phone shop was able use my existing number, thus saving me countless headaches in sorting out all my business cards and contact lists. It wasn't a surprise to find I'd loads of missed messages waiting when I turned on my new cell.

I know this is boring reading, but sometimes life is boring and full of mundane tasks we have to complete in order to keep moving forward. Let's call it a bread and butter moment, one of those times where events are used as non-substantive filler.

At eleven o'clock, I was turning into Emily's drive. I grinned at seeing her waiting for me. It felt good to have someone waiting for me, although I certainly realised that it was not in the romantic "I need you" sense. I was just giving her a lift; it was a pairing of necessity. The grin I sported as I drove to the Dogs Trust was a little forced.

Emily was chatty at first, but I think she lost the will to be companionable when my answers remained monosyllabic. It wasn't as if I ever was a chatterbox when we were together, but even I noticed my conversation lacked sparkle and va va voom.

Charlie was pleased to see us, and, after his initial greeting, he ran to the door, his tail wagging in anticipation of a good walk ahead.

The forty-five minutes flew by, and before I knew it, we were once again saying our farewells to the little chap. I didn't want to leave him there. Before I had a chance to block it out, the image of Toby at the vet's slipped inside my head. An ache wove its way from my ribcage to my throat. *Not now. Please. Not now.*

"You okay?" Emily's hand slipped through my arm, and I didn't flinch from the energy that flowed from her to me, from me to her.

"I'm great." So why did my voice sound so flat?

"Are you—"

"Hey, sis!"

Aw fuck. I should've known.

"Fancy seeing you here at this time."

Abbie's grinning face made me want to throttle her. My teeth clamped together so loudly, I was positive Emily must've heard the clack. But Abbie didn't take the hint.

"I thought you came later than this."

As if. She knew damn well I had come earlier the previous day. I had the scars from her personal Spanish Inquisition to prove it.

"Oh...hello, Emily. I didn't see you there."

Yeah, right. She didn't see the woman standing at least four inches taller than me, holding my arm, facing her.

Well, Emily had been holding my arm. Her warm fingers

slipped away, leaving a cold patch where her body had been in contact with mine.

"Oh, hi, Abbie. I thought I told you we were coming earl—"

"So glad I met up with the both of you."

Had my sister just cut Emily off? Emily had told her? My sister and Emily were having conference calls? My eyes pinned a fidgeting Abbie, and I mouthed "You fuckster," but she laughed nervously and ignored me.

"It's Rob's birthday next week, and I'm throwing a party for him this Saturday night."

And? NO! No, no, and no.

"I just wanted to make sure you could come, Emily."

Once again—NO! She was doing it again. She was trying to fix me up. This was the first I'd heard of Abbie throwing Rob a party. He hated parties.

"We would love to have you there, wouldn't we, Ellie?'"

I just glared.

"It's nothing big, like, not even a party, so you don't have to get dolled up."

See? Not even a party. I wouldn't be surprised if she invited Cherie to come, so I would feel like a double dickhead.

"I'd love to." Emily's voice was so warm, so happy, that when she turned to me and said, "If that's okay with you, Ellie." I couldn't say "Like fuck it is," like I wanted to.

"Of course. It will be a night to remember." You could bet it would be, too, if Abbie had anything to do with it.

"Aunty Wellie, look! Jessie wants to say hello!" Grinning her gap toothed grin, Lily was holding the lead to a very excited Jack Russell. "Wanna walk her wiv me?"

This was not the time to tell my sister what I thought of her scheme. The words I wanted to whisper through gritted teeth should never be in earshot of a six-year-old.

"Sorry, hon. Gotta go to work." I ruffled her hair, making her laugh. "And hello there, Poppy."

"Jessie."

The dog whined with excitement and stood on her back legs to greet me.

"You are a pearl, aren't you, *Poppy*?" I lowered my face to accept kisses from the pooch, sniggering at the overzealous attention I was receiving. I could hear Abbie talking to Emily, but their words were too soft for me to make out. That didn't keep me from knowing my sister was up to no good.

I dropped Emily at her house and didn't even linger to be invited inside. I could sense she wanted to say something, but I didn't give her the opportunity. I spluttered something about work waiting and needing to get going.

It was true. I was busy. Too many jobs and not enough hours in the day, especially if I was to take on the job for the woman who was campaigning for Dog Owner of the Year by Saturday morning.

Sorry. That sounded bitchy, I know. But my life used to be so simple. Work. Home. Eat. Shower. Bed. Then the same the next day...and the next and...ad infinitum.

Shit. Saturday morning, I was supposed to start working for Emily Carson. She would be my employer, and then I would have to be sociable when I was with her. I know taking Charlie out for a walk could be classified as being sociable, but it wasn't. I said it before and I'll say it again—it was necessity.

Who was I trying to kid? Myself? So it seemed.

The day continued in a whirl of planting and making appointments to meet with prospective clients. I made a booking to speak to a Mr Davies the following day at 11, and only suffered a little pang of guilt when I thought of Emily's face when I told her I wouldn't be joining her to see Charlie on her next visit.

You are probably very much aware that I am lying at this precise moment, aren't you?

I felt a lot of guilt, especially because it wasn't imperative that I meet with him at that time, although if you were to speak to Mr Davies, you might think that 11 was absolutely the only time slot I had available, as I had made him believe.

All afternoon, the guilt gnawed at me. I needed to tell Emily that I had changed our appointment, but I was delaying the inevitable. It wasn't as if I wouldn't get to see Charlie, that was a given. I couldn't not go and see him. A little voice kept whispering, "But you want to see her, too, don't you?"

I growled and thunked my spade into the ground, following that with a hefty stomp of my dirt covered boot. Being with Charlie was different. Making a commitment to him was so totally unlike making an arrangement with Emily. I hoped that he would become part of my family, something Emily would never be. Yes. She was attractive, and yes, I was attracted to her. But I didn't want to feel she had the upper hand in the decision about where Charlie was to live. If she thought I felt something for her, maybe she would use that to my disadvantage.

It was surprising how time spent digging in the cold hard soil could give a woman a sense of perspective, fucked up though it might be. I was being irrational. Spending time with Emily didn't mean squat unless I allowed myself to be manipulated.

Whoa. Hold them metaphorical horses a minute. Would Emily manipulate any situation? Images of her leapt into my mind—

her warm smile and soulful eyes, the sound of her laugh, the way she tossed her head back to move her fringe from her face. That didn't sound like the actions of a woman on the take. And she had seemed genuinely concerned earlier. She had slipped her hand through my arm to check how I was feeling; she had offered the lead to me and let me have my time with Charlie. It even seemed as if she wanted to spend time with me.

Aw shit. I fucked up.

I called Mr Davies and tried to change the appointment, but he had made other plans. Apparently, as soon as I'd hung up the phone, he'd made arrangements for everything from a doctor's appointment to having his hair cut. I did try, honestly. But...no. He couldn't do it at any time other than 11, when I should've been picking up Emily. At one point, I even contemplated telling him that I couldn't take the job on, but in this economy a person couldn't afford to turn down work. At least I couldn't.

So that, as they say, was that.

For the rest of the day, I kept taking out Emily's card and attempting to call her to explain, but I found out that I was, in fact, a spineless fucker who couldn't seem to get beyond the first three digits of her number. Eventually I sent her a text explaining what'd happened, and I cringed as I pressed the "send" button.

Ten minutes later I received a reply assuring me that the change in our plan was okay, and I was a little disappointed. One minute I was trying my damnedest to distance myself from Emily, and the next I was fucked off because my agonizing was not shared. Go me, and my lack of ability to understand myself, never mind anyone else understanding me.

Five minutes later, I received a second text asking, "Have I upset you?"

No. I've upset myself. Instead of answering straight away,

I did the British thing—I made a cuppa. Instead of stewing the tea, I stewed in my own thoughts. Emily hadn't done anything wrong, so why would she think I would be upset with her? I was a business woman with commitments that sometimes couldn't be avoided—or sometimes could, but I made out they couldn't—so why…

The ringing of my cell phone made me slop my tea over my fingers and swear out loud. I wasn't even surprised to see the name that flashed on the screen: "Abbie Home."

Maybe it was coincidence.

"Why have you cancelled seeing Emily tomorrow?"

"How did—"

"Why?" she persisted. "Is it because I invited her to Rob's bash?"

Bash? What the fuck?

"If you must know, I like the girl." Girl?

"It would be good to have her over so she can see that you come from a good home. She shouldn't have to just base her opinions on the picture of you that you've presented."

What did she... "Hey!"

"If you want her to give up her claim on Charlie, then you'd better toe the line."

Shit. I'd been bollocked by my big sister. "I've got a meeting with a client, if you must know." Her harrumph made me grind my teeth. "And why did you wait to ask her to come to Rob's bash until she was with me? It's obvious you two are talking on the fucking phone to each other."

"Ah...erm...we're not."

"Bye, sis." End of call.

Before Abbie could call me back, I called Emily's number without even pausing to deliberate. "Em? Hi. Ellie Anderson."

Why had I introduced myself in full, and why had I called her Em? I didn't give her a chance to get past the hello stage before I launched into another mini life story, almost a "Day in the Life Of." All she could get out in between was "erm" and "okay," followed by an "I see." Eventually I stopped rambling and let the woman talk.

"Did you want me to go and see Charlie on my own tomorrow then?"

Huh? Hadn't she been listening to my explanation? I thought I'd summed it up quite well.

"I could, erm, go later. I don't have to go at eleven."

Shit. I hadn't thought of that. I'm surprised I can actually walk and talk at the same time.

"Three?" Was I too eager? And does anyone actually give a shit?

Emily's laugh filtered through the phone, and, for some stupid girly reason, I had the urge to hug the plastic electronics to my chest.

"That would be fantastic. Maybe after we've been to the Trust, you could give me some ideas of what you plan to do first when you start making my garden presentable."

"Sure thing." Was I turning American on my own ass? Obviously, as I would have said "arse." When I said my goodbyes, I positively felt lighter. And I didn't exactly know why.

The night was full of dreams, wild dreams, dreams that were not nice at all. I woke up bathed in sweat, got up, and tried to do some invoices. I couldn't concentrate. Echoes of the dreams kept flitting through my head. An ache thrummed in my chest as images of Toby mingled with the looks from my parents as I had packed boxes into my car and left home. Why I'd dreamed about them, I don't know. It had been years since I'd allowed them to infiltrate any part of my life—conscious or subconscious. Toby, I could understand, but them? No. They meant nothing to me.

I left the house before six a.m. and got started with work. Eleven o'clock came around too quickly, as I hadn't really given myself to think about anything but work. It was too painful to keep dwelling on past events. Work was a no-brainer, something I could do without thinking too much. In other words—safe. The meeting with Mr Davies went smoothly enough, and I bagged the job. It wasn't a difficult one—he just wanted a pond put in his back garden, somewhere where he could sit with his wife when the weather became warmer. Seeing him with his wife made me regret being fucked off with him the previous day. Even though they had been together for over fifty years, love still radiated from them. Imagine being with the same person for all that time and loving them just as strongly as when you first met. I know I was not privy to their life in full, but it was apparent that those two were meant to be together.

For a fleeting moment, I wanted that. I wanted to be content, to be happy, and to be madly in love with the same person for the majority of my life. I wanted a fish pond life.

At a quarter to three, I was arriving at Emily's. Not surprisingly, she was already waiting. A little part of me wanted her to comment about me being early again, just so I could say "And you are waiting," so I could hear her musical laugh again. However, I didn't. I just grinned idiotically while pointing at my watch. Couldn't help myself. Couldn't resist seeing if I could make her laugh. When she did, my stomach flip flopped like a prize pancake.

Before long, we were out walking with the furry little tyke. This time we decided to take him to the village instead of through the woods. Charlie loved all the attention he was getting from everyone who saw him, plenty of head rubs and paw shakes to last him the rest of the day. When we walked past a shop where he caught sight of his reflection in the front window, he stopped, his neck went rigid and his ears stuck out comically.

"Woof!" His head flicked back as he must've thought the "other" dog had barked in response.

"Woof!" A little deeper, but this time he lowered his head as if he was sussing out the situation. He tentatively stepped forward and pressed his face against the glass. Swipe. A very pink tongue came out and licked his reflection, again and again. He was totally getting into it, but it was apparent my lad didn't have a case of canine narcissism—he was showing us he knew it was a reflection. Bless his adorably furry paws.

I know you are probably thinking "WTF?" but if I have to listen to straight people telling me "comical" stories about their kids, I am definitely entitled to return the favour.

The walk seemed shorter than usual, although it took the same length of time. Instead of remaining quiet, like we usually did, I had bitten the bullet and asked her something more than her age. Listening to her chatter about her business, I soon realised we were not dissimilar. Not once did she mention socialising, friends, or even the last time she had eaten out. The last bit burrowed itself inside my head and insisted, Ask her out for something to eat.

No. Thankfully the answer was internal too.

The internal voice became more persistent. Ask her!

No! I turned and grinned at Emily. You know the look, the one that screams, "Dickhead Alert!"

This time my internal voice apparently decided it was through being coy, as it drew in a huge mouthful of metaphorical air and bellowed, For fuck's sake! Ask her!

"No!" I bellowed in return.

Emily jumped.

So did I.

Charlie stopped sniffing the extremely interesting blade of grass and turned and flashed me a "What?" before eating the grass. Even my dog was telling me eating was a good thing.

"What?"

I tried for innocent. "Nothing."

"You shouted 'no'."

"Did I?" I couldn't exactly admit to my inner dialogue? "I... erm...I said 'oh'." And that is better, how?

"So, why 'oh'?"

Was this a rap? "I was just..." my eyes flicked about, finally landing on a woman across the street walking her dog, "warning you about the dog over there." Fuck-ing lame. Lame, shameful lame.

Emily looked over at the tiny Yorkshire Terrier and back at me, her frown showing her confusion.

"You can't be too careful with those dogs. They will tear your ankles off in a heartbeat."

After another glance at the miniscule dog, Emily snorted, and then laughed. "Have you seen the size of it? My ankle is bigger than its mouth."

Charlie lifted his head and sniffed the air, then turned and gave the Yorkie a glare.

I was embarrassed. And when I get embarrassed, it is guaranteed that I will do something even more stupid—like dropping my phone in the toilet. "Fancy grabbing a bite to eat after we take Charlie back?"

Emily stopped laughing and looked at me as if she was trying to work me out. If she did, I really hoped she would let me in on her discoveries.

It seemed as if time stopped, and I was the only one experiencing the stillness. Nothing around us moved, apart from Emily's hair, which wisped deliciously around her face.

"I'd love to."

Bam. Time started again, then stopped when she flashed me her crooked grin. She turned away from me and tugged Charlie's lead, making him trot beside her.

I stood for a few moments and watched her walk away, my heart hammering in my chest.

It was only a pub meal, but the thought was there. After Emily had agreed to eat with me, and we'd taken Charlie back to the kennels, I couldn't think of anywhere half decent to go without it seeming too much like a date. It wasn't a date; it was food. Good food, but still only sustenance, and a necessity. People had to eat after all; it didn't hurt to share a meal with another human being.

Who was I kidding? Being with Emily over spaghetti carbonara was totally satisfying. Watching her expertly wind the spaghetti around her fork was becoming addictive, and it was only the attraction of her eyes, her voice, her smell, the way she tucked her hair behind her ear when she was talking that distracted me. I'm lying. It wasn't just that; it was everything about her. Even the way she wiped her mouth on her napkin or sipped at her fruit juice.

Bollocks. What was happening to me? I didn't want this. But I did. God, I did. I felt myself staring at her lips, feeling exposed, feeling vulnerable, experiencing feelings I had never felt in the whole of my life before that moment. I ached to feel the softness of her lips, longed to press softly, gently, tease her mouth with the tip of my tongue, allow her breath to mingle with mine before I truly tasted her.

"You okay?"

Heat flooded my face and I clasped at my drink, raising it up to cover half my face. "I'm great. Why?"

A smile slipped over her face before she softly said, "Nothing."

By the time we got back to Emily's house, it was too dark for me to look around and make suggestions for her upcoming renovations. Instead of bidding her farewell in the car, I got out and walked her to her front door. Standing there in the light coming from her security lamp, I felt like a teenager delivering her date home after a night out. All that was needed to complete the image was a kiss at the doorstep.

I felt awkward. I wanted to kiss her—too much. I wanted to take her into my arms and show her how much I wanted to kiss her, but...but... Charlie. Would she think I was only doing this because I wanted him? Was I actually only interested in her because of him?

It was as if someone had sneaked up behind me and chucked a bucket of ice cold water over the moment.

"Eleven tomorrow, okay?" I asked. Had she always been standing so close to me? Did her eyes always seem so intense? And why didn't she answer? "Or three, like today?"

"What?" Whatever she'd been thinking about was suddenly supplanted by the realisation that she had missed what I had said. "Three, like today?"

"Three it is, then." I stepped back, not quite ready to relinquish the moment. "Thank you for tonight. I really enjoyed it."

Before she had time to respond, I was gone.

Chapter Five

Lying in bed, I thought through what had transpired earlier. Was the attraction I felt one-sided? Judging by the way Emily was looking at me as I was yearning to kiss her, I didn't think so. Maybe it was shock? Disgust? Repulsion? But no. I was positive that she was going to kiss me. So what did I do?" As usual, I was at a loss when it came to women. Don't get me wrong—I had dated a few, but none of them had made me feel the way Emily did.

Shit. I didn't need this. I didn't want this. I just wanted to feel nothing, like I usually did. Allowing a woman into my life was not conducive to my lifestyle. I wanted it to be me and my dog, and that way...that way... That way, what? I wouldn't ever again have to see someone I cared about turn their back on me like my parents had? Wouldn't ever again have to detach myself from the life I had known and change everything I had thought was part and parcel of my life?

Shit. Again. Why was I thinking about them? They meant nothing to me, just as I meant nothing to them.

Still, it wouldn't hurt to have a new friend to do things with.

An evil grin spread over my face as a smug thought popped into my head. A new friend who might want to walk MY dog with ME.

Nestling down under my duvet, I conjured up images of Charlie chasing his ball. A warm feeling spread through me and my heart lifted, which was a surprise, as I hadn't realised it had sunk.

Shall I say shit for the third time? Looks like it.

Why was I suddenly too aware of my bodily functions, especially that organ in my chest, just to the left of centre?

I threw off the covers, deciding sleep would not be coming easily after all.

Because I had gone into work so early every day, I completed the current job before lunch so decided to go home and shower before going to pick up Emily. I spent an amazingly long time on deciding what to wear, but as soon as I realised I was doing it, I just slipped into my favourite jeans and a sweater.

Emily was waiting at the gate, her grin glorious. She looked beautiful. It was then that it struck me: Why would Emily like me anyway? I wasn't anything special. Granted, I wasn't a minger, but I wasn't on the same plane as Emily Carson. She was stunning, especially when she smiled. Why on earth was she still single when it was obvious she could have had anyone she wanted?

"I hope you don't mind, but I have to get straight back after we walk Charlie."

I was busy faffing about with my seat to follow up on her remark, so I grunted a response.

"I have a friend coming around later."

That stopped me in my tracks. A friend? She hadn't mentioned "a friend" when we had been chatting the previous evening.

I turned to look at her and saw her blush before she looked sheepishly out of the side window. Clink. Penny dropping again. That kind of friend...as in either girlfriend, ex-girlfriend, or potential girlfriend. A wave of disappointment swamped me.

"Okay. Sure thing." I started the engine. "If you can't come, it's —"

"No! Erm...no. I have plenty of time."

I nodded. So, even though I'd already decided Emily was too good for me and, also, if I'd had a shot, I would have preferred to be one of those friends without benefits, I was still feeling gutted.

See? Life is a bitch, even when you've declared that you didn't want anything more than you already had.

Saturday morning came around, and I didn't want to go to work. It was unusual for me to feel that way. Ever since I had left home, work seemed the only thing I had going for me in my life—except for Toby and Abbie.

But, I had to. After all, Emily was expecting me.

I turned up at her place just after eight and was a little disappointed not to see Emily waiting for me at the gate. She wasn't sanding her window sills either. I couldn't see her anywhere. Sighing, I moved around to the back of my pickup and started to unload my tools.

"Good morning." The voice came from behind me, a voice I

didn't recognise. "You must be Ellie."

Turning, I saw a woman in her thirties—a very good looking woman, who was grinning at me and holding out her free hand in greeting. The other was cradling a coffee cup. "I'm Michelle Simmons, a...friend of Emily's."

The friend, eh? The friend who had so obviously spent the night. And by the glow on her face, the friend who'd had a very fulfilling night full of sex. A flush gathered on my face as I envisioned Emily in the throes of passion with the blonde standing before me. If I hadn't been feeling a sharp stab of jealousy plunging into me, I would have admitted they made a wonderful image. Two stunning women loving each other.

"It is Ellie, isn't it? Ems said you would be here today."

My eyes flicked to her outstretched hand, and I realised I had completely ignored her gesture. It wasn't her fault that she was the cat that got the cream.

"Oh...yes...sorry. I was miles away there. Ellie Anderson." I was almost fawning, the act of the bitter love rival hiding her feelings. I know what you're thinking—one minute I wanted Emily, and the next I didn't. Couple that with the jealousy, and you have me in the bag—a fucked up loner with tickets on and off herself.

A laugh spluttered out of her mouth, and she grabbed my hand and started pumping it up and down. As her body came closer to mine, I caught the distinct scent of Emily's perfume. Could things get any worse?

"Do you need a hand unloading? Emily's in the shower as she overslept this morning." Michelle leaned closer and gave me a wink. "She hasn't got the stamina she used to have."

Looked like a "yes" on the things-getting-worse question.

"No. I'm fine. Honestly." I wanted to flee the scene, as I

didn't want to find out any more about what had happened between Emily and Michelle. "There's one thing you could do, if you don't mind."

Michelle's face turned serious as she nodded and stood straight, at mock attention.

"Could you tell Emily I'll be back later? I have to pick up some supplies."

A frown flitted over her beautiful face before she said, "We were hoping you could join us for breakfast."

Fuck that! I produced my most charming grin. "Sorry again. I've already eaten." I hadn't, but she didn't know that. "I'll be back after lunch."

Before Michelle had chance to say anything, my phone sounded. "Got to get this. Sorry." Why was I repeatedly apologising to her?

Michelle smiled and nodded at the screaming phone in my hand.

I turned my face away from her and clicked "accept." "Hey, baby, how're you this morning?"

"What? You pissed?" Abbie didn't sound like she was going to play along, but I didn't care.

"I was going to wake you, but you were flat out."

"You are pissed. And fucking crazy. What's—"

"Seven? That would be wonderful."

"You're fucking me off now. What's—"

"Got to go. Work beckons." I held the "end call" button slightly longer than I needed to so the phone would turn off completely. There was one thing in this world that I was sure about at that moment, and it was that my sister would call me straight back.

I turned back to Michelle and was momentarily frozen by

the look on her face. It was a look of disappointment. Or had I imagined it? It was so fleeting, maybe I had. Shrugging, I said, "Women, eh?"

Michelle nodded. "So...erm... I'll leave you to get on with your work then." Without another word, she was gone, the cup dangling from her hand.

When I returned to Emily's at one, Michelle was not in sight and, once again, Emily was not outside. Instead of announcing my arrival, I unloaded the fence panels and posts I'd bought to make the perimeter safer. Still no sign of Emily, even though I knew she had to be there.

I didn't want to go and knock on the door in case they were inside reliving the events of the previous evening. But Charlie would be waiting. We were past our usual time. He would think we had abandoned him.

The more I thought about Charlie waiting at the bars of his kennel, looking for us, the more antsy I became. Why was I avoiding Emily? It wasn't as if she wasn't entitled to a love life. Just because she didn't want me that way shouldn't affect any-thing. Our relationship was a business arrangement, involving her garden and the eventual ownership of the main man himself.

After twenty minutes, I decided to get a spine and knock. What could be the worst that could happen? Scrap that com-ment. Knowing my luck, I would interrupt them getting jiggy with it on the kitchen table.

In answer to my knock, Emily's voice invited me inside. She was on the phone. She mouthed "hello" and followed that with a mischievous grin. "Yes. Yes. She's here now. You want to talk to her?"

Huh? Who would call Emily and then want to speak to me? I knew the answer to that even before I took the phone from her, and my heart plummeted to my stomach before bouncing back up and jamming in my throat.

"Thought I'd get you this way. What the hell are you up to now?" Abbie's voice held a hint of humour.

She knew damned well what I'd been up to. I hoped she'd kept it to herself and not gobbed off to Emily. I didn't need my sister to make me look like an idiot; I was more than capable of doing that for myself.

"Never mind," she said.

That was a first. When Abbie wanted answers, she didn't give up easily.

"I'll see you later." She waited a beat and then added, "You can tell me then." A gargling noise came from my mouth, but Abbie had the upper hand. "Or do you want me to tell Emily you pretended you have a love life?"

"Seven will be great! Can't wait to see you!"

"Good girl. You know I know best."

After hanging up the phone, I turned to see Emily standing in the doorway, her coat draped over her arm. "Ready?"

Although on first look, Emily seemed her usual self, bubbly and gorgeous, there was something missing from her smile. It wasn't vivacious, wasn't as full and true and totally engaging as I had come to expect.

"Sure."

What did you expect me to do? Ask her what was wrong?

It wasn't until we were halfway to the Trust that I realised why Emily was not herself. Michelle. It was obvious. I hadn't seen Michelle, and Emily was more than likely missing her. At that point, I started to chew my lip. Should I have invited Michelle to come with us instead of surmising everything should be exactly the same as all the other times we had gone to visit Charlie? Was I being selfish? Indifferent? Or was I just being me?

"Are you missing Michelle?" WTF? I didn't want to talk about her girlfriend. Nearly anything but. I didn't turn to look at her when she answered. I didn't want to see the longing on her face.

"Yes. I always do when she's not about."

Considering last night was the first I knew about her girlfriend, I found that surprising.

"I rarely get to see her nowadays."

Or rarely bring her up in conversation, so it seems. God, I'm a bitch.

"It's been over a year since the last time."

"What the fuck! Over a year?" It popped out. Couldn't stop it. But a year without seeing your other half? Doesn't that seem a little long to you?

Emily laughed aloud. "I understand. She's busy. Her work takes her everywhere."

But a year?

"And now she's got Tania, too, so now I have to share her."

Who the fuck was Tania and what, exactly, did she mean by sharing? I glanced at her and saw that she was grinning. Was it just me that believed if you were in a relationship, it should be just the two of you and you should see each other more than once a year?

"I wonder if Charlie thinks we're not coming."

How could she talk about Charlie when her girlfriend was doing more than the hokey cokey with another woman?

"Erm. I guess." Looks like I was going to keep my thoughts to myself.

I think in his own furry little way, Charlie didn't think we were going to turf up at all. If you could have seen the way his eyes lit up, the way he grabbed and shook his tuggy rope and fought it all the way over to us—accompanied by mewling growls—you would have agreed with me that he was excited. Lots of kissing and licks followed his initial display, and I have to admit I felt well and truly loved and welcomed. I'd known him less than a week, and I felt as if my life couldn't function properly without him in it.

A voice inside my head trickled through my brain, down my spine, and spread out through my body. An insistent voice saying it wasn't just Charlie that was making me feel that way. It was also the woman with the long distance, two-timing girlfriend. A sigh slipped out, but I tried to hide it by getting Charlie even more excited than he already was.

"You can let him off the lead today if you feel brave enough." Sharon was standing at the side of the door, an encouraging grin on her face. "His leg is getting better, and a little time off the lead won't hurt him at this stage in his recovery."

"Really?" Emily sounded thrilled.

I felt scared shitless. What if he ran off? Got hit by a car? Saw a squirrel and thought it more interesting than us? What if his leg went? What if—

"You okay?" Emily sounded concerned.

"As much as I would like to..." I found it hard to finish the excuse, as I knew it was lame.

"Come on. Take a risk. How will we know what he is capable of if we never give him a chance?"

Risk or chance. The same thing, but completely opposite. One sounded positive, whereas the other saw me without Charlie in my life.

Emily was staring at me.

I wanted to be like her, wanted to be a chance taker, let my lad run through the grass and smell the freedom.

"If you love something, let it go."

Was that the best she could come up with? If I loved something, I held it close, and didn't fuck off for twelve months at a time. Maybe that was her style, but it certainly wasn't mine.

"I'd prefer if we waited a little longer, if you don't mind." I patted Charlie's head. "I don't want to risk it just yet." Story of my life, really. Risk equals loss in my book. I'd risked telling my parents about me not being the straight, grandkid-bearing daughter they had raised, and look where that had gotten me. I risked loving Toby as much as I had, and look what happened there. I'd also taken a risk by allowing Emily Carson into my life...

I want to stop there. I think I've made my point.

I dropped Emily off and went home to shower and change before what was now termed as "Rob's Bash." I was going to suggest I pick her up and take her there, but I stopped myself. Asking her if she wanted a lift to my sister's opened too many doors to too many rooms that I wasn't willing to visit. Emily had a girlfriend, and I was just the other woman who wanted Charlie as much— although I would say more—as she did. It was for the best. For me. I had to clarify that last bit as I would hate you to believe that Emily Carson had, at any point in our budding relationship, actually believed that we would move toward something more. I think I'm going off the point, or just maybe rambling. Again.

Six-forty-five saw me knocking on Abbie's door.

Instead of it being opened by the toothless wonder, Lily, I found myself greeted by none other than the Queen of Sheba herself. "Where's Em?" she asked.

"Hi to you too. Good to see you." My sarcasm was lost on Abbie, so I held up the bags with wine and nibbles. "I come bearing offerings from the great God Tesco."

"Didn't you pick her up as we arranged?"

"We?" I didn't remember me being involved in the "we" part."

Excited screams came from the lounge and I would really like to say it was Rob, but it was my niece.

"Maybe you should go and get her if you love her so much." Before she could respond, I pushed past Abbie and called out to the rugrat.

Lily came bounding down the hallway, her arms outstretched and ready for me to pick her up and fling her about before lavishing her with kisses. "Where's Em?"

Was this a conspiracy? Even my six year old niece was turning Spanish Inquisitor.

"Me wants to see Em too."

For fuck's sake! Turning my head, I was greeted by serious green eyes and a pouting mouth.

"You get her for me."

I opened my mouth to say no, but she placed her finger over my lips and shook her head. "You get her for me. Please?"

Shit. They were definitely working me over. Talk about a guilt trip. Why had it suddenly become my responsibility to bring Emily to the party? "She's probably already on her way here, baby."

Blond eyebrows quirked, but her gaze was constant.

"Emily is coming here on her own, Lils."

A cough from behind me broke Lily's stare, and Abbie spoke. "Erm...well...maybe she is waiting for you."

I shook my head. "I left her at her house with no mention of picking her up." I placed Lily on the floor, and she automatically gripped my leg and started hanging from my jeans. "Why would she be waiting for me?"

At least my sister had the grace to look embarrassed. "I called her about an hour ago and told her you would."

"What the fu—"

"Bad word, Aunty Wellie."

My teeth clonked together and the air shot from both nostrils.

"I did leave you a message on your mobile. Didn't you get it?"

Duh! Well, it looked like a resounding "no" from here.

Lily was tugging me towards the door in the hopes I would get the message and bugger off to pick up her new friend.

I wanted to be all pissy and say I hadn't heard the phone ring, but I knew, and so did Abbie, that I hadn't turned my mobile back on since the morning, when I was pretending to be talking to some woman other than my sister. That also reminded me that Abbie had one on me.

"What time did you say I would be there?" What else could I do? Abbie, as always, had the upper hand. Don't get me wrong, my sister would defend me to the death, but it didn't mean that she wouldn't have fun with me when she could. To spend the evening walking on eggshells was not what I wanted. If you'd ever been the victim of my sister's piss taking, you would've caved too.

Fifteen minutes later, I was pulling up outside Emily's, and wasn't surprised to see her waiting outside and on the phone. I knew she was talking to my sister even before she said she would see her in a little while. It was the grin. Part of me wondered what Abbie had said to her, but the bigger part of me didn't want to know.

"You look beautiful." I think the words that came out of her mouth surprised her even more than they did me. The blush spread over her face as if she had been frantically airbrushed. "I mean, erm...I usually only see you in your work gear."

No I didn't, and she knew I didn't. Her blush turned incandescent. I grinned but didn't respond to her compliment. The door opened and she eased herself inside, the smell of her perfume filling my senses. God, she smelled good. She always smelled good, but tonight the scent was even more intoxicating.

I watched her fiddle with her seatbelt, trying to get it to slip into the slot, the strong, slender fingers fumbling around the clasp.

"Here. Let me." Click. Not just the seatbelt, but something else too.

It was as if time slowed down once again as my eyes drifted from her hands to her wrists to her arm, across her chest and up her throat. I saw her swallowing rapidly and wished I, too, could swallow. My gaze was fixed on her soft red lips, parted slightly, almost waiting. Brown eyes seemed bottomless, like swirling melted chocolate.

"There. There you go." It was agony tearing myself away from her; I could almost feel the splitting. I gripped the steering wheel hard to stop the shaking in my hands. It was almost as if I had no control over my body.

"Thank you."

For the rest of the drive, we were quiet. There were so many things I wanted to say to her, but none of them were about Charlie or the work I was going to do on her land. I wanted to ask her why she put up with Michelle's infidelity, why she didn't see her for months on end, why—and this was the big one—why she made me feel so fucking much. But I kept quiet, kept my self-serving questions to myself.

When we arrived, Lily was waiting outside, pretending to bounce her ball against the wall.

As soon as I pulled up the handbrake, she was next to Emily's side of the car, trying to open the door.

"Me told Aunty Wellie to git you."

Aw fuck.

"And Mummy did."

Anything else, Lily? Do you want to grass me up about my swearing too?

"She said a bad word."

Looked like a "yes." I tried the forced chortling to negate Lily's statements. "Kids, eh?" Forced snorting made me seem like the village idiot. "I didn't say a bad word, Lils." I'd stopped, hadn't I? I'd only got the "fu" out.

Emily turned to me and a fleeting glimpse of disappointment flashed over her face.

"I wouldn't swear in front of a child. Honestly." Maybe I should have crossed my fingers on that one.

A small smile appeared on Emily's face. "I believe you."

Thousands wouldn't have, myself included. So, if she believed me, why did she still have that look of disappointment on her face? Sometimes I can be as thick as shit.

The evening went better than I had anticipated. Thankfully, Abbie had invited other people so it didn't look as if it was just a ruse to get Emily and me together. Another bonus was that there was no sign of Cherie. Result! An additional surprise was that Abbie didn't try to match make—although I was expecting it all night and found myself analysing everything she said or did. As for Lily—she was infatuated with Emily, and I think Emily was a little taken with my niece, too, truth be told. There are not many people who would make such a fuss over a six-year-old, even to the extent of playing dolls with her. I mean—dolls! Who plays with dolls now? Especially dolls that insist on having tea parties where the "dolls" chat about Justin Bieber, Jessie J, and One Direction. I have to admit, Emily did well. She even smiled like she meant it when she found herself performing a duet of Never Say Never with a bit of Price Tag blended in for original-ity.

But you know what? At one point I was really hoping Abbie would push us together. I know. I know! Emily had a girlfriend, and I wouldn't be the one to make her "do a Michelle." I knew I wasn't two-timing quality. And her having a girlfriend wasn't the only reason, as you well know. I didn't want this, didn't want to get involved whether Emily had a bird or not.

Just because Emily was attractive—well, to be truthful, beautiful—that didn't mean I should pursue her because of what was commonly known as "cosmetics." That was shallow. And just because I found myself looking over at her time and time again, that didn't mean anything. It was the way she laughed.

The problem was the way the sound of it drifted over to me and distracted me from conversing with Rob's mates. It didn't mean anything that excitement raced through my body every time she looked my way, every time she blessed me with a smile.

In the end, I decided I would help tidy up. Being in the kitchen with a sink full of pots was just what I needed to ground me. Abbie and Rob took turns reminding me that I was a guest and was missing out on the party. Don't get me wrong, I didn't spend all my time at the sink. I did find myself drifting over to the door to see what was happening in the throng of it all. I found myself searching out a certain pair of brown eyes, but I still wouldn't allow myself to stroll down anything beyond the street of attraction.

It was twelve-thirty by the time the party drew to a close. Lily had been in bed ever since she had flopped face first onto the sofa at approximately ten o'clock. I was surprised she had lasted as long as she had considering her throat must've been caning her after all the high notes she had attempted. I knew it was down to me to take Emily home, as I had been the one to deliver her earlier, however grudgingly. I was thrumming with excitement as I knew it would just be her and me. Alone. In the cab of my truck. And what rhymes with truck? Begins with "f". Yep. That big old swear word that was rapidly becoming the word that came to mind when I thought of myself alone with Emily Carson.

"Did you have a good night?" Civilised, don't you think?

Emily emitted a chuckle followed by a long breath. "Is your niece always so musical?"

It was my turn to chuckle. I shook my head.

"I mean...Bieber, Jessie, and... Who the hell is One Direction?"

I laughed out loud.

"In some screwed up way, I feel abused." There was humour was in her tone, and it made me feel all warm inside.

"Who cares who they are?" A soft laugh escaped her. I could almost feel the sensation of it touching my skin.

The rest of the journey was quiet, just the sound of the truck's engine and the tyres moving along the road, but it wasn't uncomfortable. No. It was safe, warm, companionable. We didn't need to talk; it was perfect just the way it was.

As I pulled up outside Emily's house, I felt her absence even before she got out of the car. In a screwed up way, I wanted her to just leave as quickly as possible, almost like ripping off a plaster to get the pain over with. Still, I knew as soon as she slammed my truck door, I would feel the relentless sting.

Ping. The light in my cab flicked on as she opened the door. In my mental meanderings I had missed the sound of the seatbelt being unclipped. And why I even thought something as insignificant as the unclipping of a seatbelt was important is anybody's guess.

"Thank you, Ellie. Erm... I had a wonderful time."

I grinned stupidly.

"Wow. I didn't know it was so late," she said into the silence.

I knew what she was going to say next. Something along the lines of "You've kept me out too long. Goodnight."

"There's no point asking... Nah, it's gone one," she said.

Ask what? Obviously not the time, as she seemed pretty set up on that front. "What?"

Emily shook her head. "Nothing. It's okay."

It niggles me when people do that. You know, when they've said something or are thinking something and half tell you but then say it's nothing. "It can't be nothing if you were going to say it. What?"

"Erm...it's late."

"It's late? Is that what you were going to say? Doesn't seem much like a que—"

"Wouldyouliketocomeinforcoffee?"

A butterfly of excitement fluttered up my throat as I turned the engine off. She was nervous about asking me in for coffee. Coffee. The hot liquid stimulant that a person used as a ploy to get another person back to their place. What had happened to my thoughts about not wanting her to do a Michelle?

Shit. Michelle. I felt the butterfly stagger and age before stumbling over its fluttering wings. Emily was involved with someone else, so it didn't matter whether I found her desirable or not. If I knew Emily like I thought I was beginning to know her, it was only coffee being offered. And if I knew me like I knew me, I was half disappointed and half relieved.

As she was fumbling with her keys, I stood behind her grinning intermittently. I was happy to be going inside, happy that it was only a friendly nightcap, but... That's why I was grinning in stops and starts. However much I tried to convince myself I was content with just coffee, truth be told, I was gutted all down one side.

"Are you coming in, or do you want me to bring your coffee out to you?"

"No...yes. I'm coming."

She grinned at me, and I could see the sparkle of her eyes even though it was dark. Emily led me through the house to the room at the back. Inside was a sofa, a small table, and not much else. The room was starkly lit for about thirty seconds. Emily clicked on a lamp and switched off the main light that hung from the ceiling.

"Won't be a tick."

And she was gone, leaving me standing at the side of the sofa like I was frightened it would swallow me whole if I dared put my arse on it.

"Come on, Anderson," I whispered to myself. "It's coffee. Just coffee. She's got a girlfriend." I tentatively lowered myself onto the sofa, sinking backwards as soon as my butt hit the cushion.

Emily's head appeared around the door. "Would you like something stronger? Wine? Beer?"

But it was supposed to be coffee. This was a definite changing of the rules, and I wasn't savvy in the art of what to do when someone moved the goalposts.

"Better not. I'm driving." Not bad. Could have been more sophisticated, but it did show I had good morals and values.

Emily tilted her head to one side, her top lip slipping inside her mouth as she nibbled it gently in thought. When it reappeared, it was slightly wet and glistening. "You could always stay here tonight."

Stay? Stay at Emily Carson's after drinking alcohol? Stay at Emily Carson's after drinking alcohol and not long after I had realised I was very attracted to her? It was friendship suicide.

"Never mind. It was just a thought." She grinned. "Coffee it is, then."

"Wine." What? "Please."

The grin she had given me before paled in comparison to the one she gave me at that moment, and I knew I had made the right decision.

Shame I didn't feel the same way once she had gone back to the kitchen. What the fuck was I doing? It was obvious that I couldn't handle my drink—look at New Year's. That's right.

Where had my resolve to never drink again gone to? At least I had behaved myself with Cherie; no amount of alcohol could have made me climb into the sack with her. The most worrying thing to me at the moment was that I knew I didn't need to be under the influence of demon juice to happily climb into Emily's bed.

Michelle. Yes. The girlfriend. I had to keep focusing on that, and I would be fine. I wasn't the type of girl who would have a one night stand with someone who was involved with someone else, however weird I found their relationship.

Clink. I knew she was collecting two glasses and was on her way back to the room. So, like a thirteen-year-old on her first date, I scooted to the furthest corner of the sofa and waited.

"Red okay?"

I nodded and smiled coyly. I was regressing, or maybe regretting my spontaneous reaction.

"Here you go."

I had planned on sipping, but my mouth had other ideas. I had half-finished the glass before Emily had sat down. Not good.

The room was so quiet, I even wished for a clock to break the silence.

"So."

When Emily spoke, I jumped. Anyone watching through the window would have thought I was sitting with a notorious killer instead of a wonderful, gentle woman. Come to think of it, if someone was watching us through the window, I probably should have been more concerned about him.

"Tell me more about you. What do you like to do?"

When?

"You go out much? Any hobbies?"

Huh? Why couldn't I think of anything to say?

Emily turned her attention to her glass and swirled the dark red liquid. She looked lost in thought.

I couldn't help staring at her profile: straight nose, full red lips—and not from the wine, long dark lashes... The dark brown eyes were looking straight into mine.

"Anyone special in your life?"

Hopefully you.

No.

Michelle.

"I bet you have them lining up, don't you." A short laugh slipped out, and she tried to drown it with a sip of wine.

"Lining up to do what?"

The wine sprayed into the air with a pppffffffffft, followed by coughing.

I leaned over and slapped her on the back. Then again. Then once more for luck.

"Lining up to go out with you. The women. I bet you have to beat them off with a stick."

"Me? Women lining up?" Yes. Me? Women lining up? As if. I couldn't remember the last person who had showed me any interest, Cherie excluded.

"Yes. You." Emily smiled tentatively at me before turning her face away and staring at her wine again.

It must've been no more than ten seconds before I answered, but it seemed like a lot longer. If there had been a ticking clock, at least I would have had a gauge to judge by. "No. There are no lines, no sticks, and no girlfriends. And," I drained the rest of my wine, "no more wine in this glass."

Emily laughed as she shot to her feet, then scooped the glass from my outstretched hand. "Your wish is my command, master."

I wished. Whilst she was gone, I began to wonder why she had asked me if I had a girlfriend. Was it just something people did? I was so out of the loop when it came to socialising, I couldn't follow social etiquette. With Abbie, it was different. She knew everything about my life anyway. Actually, she knew more about what was going on in my life than I did. Not that it would have been a full time job to keep tabs on my boring existence. A few seconds every day would have been more than enough.

"Here you go."

My wineglass hovered in front of me, and I stared at the liquid as it sloshed about. I moved my attention to the slender fingers cupping the base of the glass and imagined them stroking my face.

"Here you go."

Or maybe the thumb, moving delicately over my lips, tantalising them with a promise of something else, something more satisfying.

"Ellie?"

Not that it would lead to anything. I would have to stop her, remind her she was already involved with someone else.

"Are you okay?"

Snap. That was me coming back to the present moment. "Erm. Yeah. Sorry." I laughed, or rather, giggled like a teenager on helium before accepting the glass from Emily's hand. "I was in a world of my own for a minute there."

"Penny for them."

I giggled my helium-filled cackle once again and then sipped my wine and nodded in approval. "Nice. Smooth." Unlike my weak attempt to change the subject.

Emily settled herself beside me, her body leaning forward,

her eyes fixed on her wine. More silence. Maybe it wasn't such a great idea after all—me coming in for wine-flavoured coffee. It was my turn to get the conversation going this time. I could feel it.

"What are your plans for the house?" Trust me to bring up the topic of work when I should have been charming the pants off her. "You keeping it, or selling it after it is finished?"

A sigh slipped from her mouth, followed shortly by a small smile. "Keeping it."

It was then that I realised I already knew that. Could I fuck up any more? "Oh, yeah. I remember now." Actually, it was not the wisest thing to admit that I had forgotten that she wanted to settle down, get a good garden space for Charlie, and have a place for her to rest her boots. It proved I was a dickhead. Time for Plan B.

"So. How long have you and Michelle been together?"

Emily's head shot around, brown eyes wide in surprise.

What? She didn't think I would bring up the topic of her girlfriend?

"Michelle and me?"

And whoever else either of them decided to bring into their lives, yes.

A short, sharp laugh. "Michelle?"

Why was she being so...so...weird?

"Michelle? As in 'this morning Michelle?'" she sputtered through another laugh.

My head bobbed rapidly; I didn't trust my voice.

"My best friend from uni Michelle? The one who is with Tania?" This time she threw her head back and bellowed.

Fuck me. It was only a question. A simple "three years" would have sufficed.

"You think I am with Michelle?"

Well, not at this precise moment, no, but the way Michelle had talked that morning... Wait. What exactly did she say that made me think she was, in fact, Emily's girlfriend? She'd said that Emily didn't have the same stamina anymore. I had, like usual, over-analysed Michelle's use of the term "friend." "Erm. Yes?"

"Michelle is with Tania. She has been for over a year."

But...

Very deliberately, Emily leaned forward and placed her wine-glass on the floor, and then turned to me. Brown eyes intently looked into mine as she pursed her lips. "I am single, Ellie. Very much so."

Single. Sin-gle. As in, not with anybody. A free agent. Up for grabs. Wait. That sounded just plain wrong. I'll change that to "available." Or should I give voice to my thought and say, "Available?"

It was the way she was looking at me, the way those choco-late eyes had changed from being so serious to almost liquid that was nearly my undoing. I wanted to lean over and brush my lips over hers and tell her how absolutely beautiful she was, but I couldn't move.

Time seemed to stand still, and the air between us was the only barrier. Her face was getting closer to mine. Was I moving towards her, or was she leaning into me? Her eyes were closing, her lips were parting, her breath was dancing over my skin.

My heart was thumping so hard I was sure she could hear it, or see it trying to force itself out of my chest to dive into her. All the moisture from my mouth evaporated, and I frantically licked my lips as if I was anticipating a delicious meal.

Emily's tongue slipped from her mouth and swiped along her

bottom lip.

She was going to kiss me. She was going to kiss me. She. Was. Going. To. Kiss. Me.

I don't know what it was inside me that made me shoot to my feet and stagger a few steps away, spilling my wine on my jeans. There was something that I hadn't known was hiding there, something I had forgotten was lurking in the depths. I realized it was fear. I knew if she kissed me right then, I would be completely lost, completely under her spell. I couldn't, just couldn't allow her to make me want her more than I wanted her already. I couldn't take the chance, couldn't risk it.

"Bathroom?"

Emily was still leaning into the spot I had occupied only a moment before. It was obvious she had fallen forward as I had made my cowardly escape. I could see the blush on her cheeks, but she wouldn't look directly at me.

"Upstairs, second door on the right."

I nodded and raced off in the direction of the stairs, carrying my wineglass with me.

I closed the bathroom door and slumped heavily against it. What was I doing? Why had I run? I wanted to kiss her so fucking badly. Still did. Why couldn't I just let her in? She wasn't my parents, wasn't Toby, wasn't all the other people in my life who had not stuck around. And Toby couldn't help it. This was Emily, the woman I was falling for. Fuck. Falling for. It wasn't love, not yet. It couldn't be love; I just really liked her. I had a case of stage fright, that was all.

I became aware of the glass of red wine still in my hand. With one swift gulp, I finished it. The heat of the liquid flowed through me, plucking up my courage and inflaming the blood in my veins. Moments later, I was back in the living room.

Emily was still seated on the sofa, but she stood as I walked in. I didn't think, didn't allow anything else to come between me and this moment. I also didn't give her the opportunity to move away, to apologise, to do anything but be pulled towards me, be pulled towards me and kissed.

Initially her lips were surprised, stiff, but I was insistent. My hand slipped around her neck and pulled her face downwards, and I became lost in the softness of her mouth. It started gently, but as the pressure of her lips increased, the world disappeared, and it was just me and Emily. Just when I felt I needed to absorb her into me, she tentatively touched my lips with her tongue, and I opened my mouth to let her inside. God. To be kissed by her. To be kissed by Emily Carson. It was all I had dreamed her kiss would be, and more besides. Her hands were slipping down my back, and I could feel the dips and peaks of each curve as her hands explored. The heat of her was melting into me, and I felt as if I was on fire.

It didn't take much pressure to push her down onto the sofa, not much effort at all to slip over her. I didn't miss a heartbeat as I cupped a perfect breast and gently squeezed it. Her moan made all the moisture from my body collect in the place that had lain dormant so long. I nudged her thighs apart and settled myself between them. Her legs wrapped around me and squeezed, pressing me deeper into her. I needed to feel her skin, needed to mould my flesh against hers. Needed to connect fully, claim all of her, scoop her up and swallow her whole. My hips began to grind against her mound, my jeans tormenting the very place I wanted her touch.

Releasing her breast, my fingers invaded the space between flesh and shirt. Cool, yet fevered skin met my touch, and I moved upwards to capture her breast through just her bra. An erect nipple strained against my palm and I rubbed, luxuriating at the feel of the peak against my hand.

"God! Ellie! Yes!" Her voice was seductive, addictive.

My lips moved to her throat and sucked, whilst my hand pushed her bra aside. Feeling her breast, the softness of it, the curve and bounce... I wanted to taste it. Wanted to move my mouth over it and claim it, devour it, become lost in it.

When I leaned back, I felt the coolness of our separation.

Brown eyes fluttered open, hooded and pleading. Her hands cupped my ass and tried to pull me back against her, but I wanted more, needed to feel more of her.

Without preamble, I tore her shirt open, the buttons skittering in all directions. The black bra was askew, one breast exposed and waiting for my mouth. It didn't have to wait long. The feel of her, the taste, the way she responded as I feasted nearly made me cum. But I wanted it all. Emily's hands dipped under my top and glided up my back, sending waves of electricity jolting through my skin. The sensation made my hips buck. Emily moaned, a long guttural moan that made me thrust harder against her. Her hips met mine, and the tempo of the dance increased. I could feel the desire building, feel the burning need to take her, plunge my fingers into her and make her mine.

Without releasing my hold on her breast, I grappled with the button on her jeans. Pop. Button gone, the zipper was fluid, as was my hand. I shifted to allow my fingers to slip inside her panties, but found myself on the outside. Her heat, her wetness, made me groan against her breast.

"Emily. Please."

What I was asking her, I don't know. Maybe I thought her underwear would miraculously disappear along with the jeans that were cramping my hand. I rubbed along her crease, and her hips jerked while her nails dug lightly into my back. Having her so open, so close, so wet and ready and not being able to take her—was agony.

Giving up the grip I had on her ass, I used that hand to tug at her jeans. Initially Emily tried to help me, but then, she stopped. It took me a few seconds to realise that my need for consummation was one-sided, and I lifted my head from her breast and met her eyes. She wasn't angry, she just seemed sad in some strange way. Why would she seem sad? Didn't she want this as much as I did? Hadn't she said yes? Called out to God? Pushed back into me as I pushed into her?

I opened my mouth to ask her, but she just shook her head. But she was so wet, so ready! I knew she had wanted me just as much as I wanted her. I could still feel her desire on the tips of my fingers. I pulled my hand out of her jeans and sat back, then climbed off her. It was time to leave. Past time, apparently.

"Ellie. Please."

I felt stupid. So fucking stupid. Why had I decided to take the bull by the horns and go with the moment?

"Goodnight, Emily."

"Ellie. Don't go. Stay. Please."

So you can lead me on again?

As my hand grasped the door handle, hers covered it. I stared at her fingers—her long, slender fingers.

"You can't leave."

I turned my head and looked into her eyes. They were so dark that the black pupils nearly swallowed the brown. "Why not, Emily? Haven't you teased me enough?" I spat.

Her lip quivered, her eyes flickered closed and then opened again. "You don't understand. I need to—"

"I understand perfectly," I ground out, grasping the door

handle.

"You've been drinking. You can't drink and drive."

I didn't know what hurt more—the way she'd led me on, or the reason she didn't want me to leave. Either way, it hurt.

"Look, I'm sorry. I didn't mean for things to get out of hand. I really like you, Ellie."

I heard the sob as her voice broke, and I felt my anger ebb.

"I don't want to be just another notch, another one night stand." Her hand lifted from mine, as if she was giving me the option to decide.

Another notch? I could barely remember the last "notch" I'd had, never mind a collection of them. As for a one night stand, that wasn't my style at all. I let my hand fall to my side.

"Come. I'll show you your room." Her hand reached out.

I started to lift mine to take hers, but stopped. Instead, I just nodded.

We didn't speak beyond just the necessities—where the bedroom was, a spare toothbrush, a t-shirt to sleep in, and then I was on my own, lying in the dark in the spare room in the house of the woman I had nearly taken on her sofa. To say sleep was difficult would have been an understatement.

Up and dressed at six-thirty, I hoped to sneak out without having to see Emily. However, she was seated at the kitchen table when I went downstairs. As soon as I entered the room, she was on her feet asking if I wanted breakfast, a coffee, anything.

I smiled as I politely declined. I just wanted to get out of there and back to the safety of my sad little life. This situation was so fucked up. Last night, before the debacle on the sofa, we had been on our way to a good solid friendship. I was supposed to be working for her, but how could I do that now? And what about Charlie? What about my little boy? We were in that together, and now I'd jeopardised him, too, with my inability to resist my wanting her.

"I'd better just get back. I've things to do." I moved towards the door. I nearly made it, too, but then she spoke again.

"Eleven, okay?"

Shit. I was just going to go by myself.

"To see Charlie?" she added by way of clarification.

I pursed my lips and gritted my teeth, before I felt I could turn and face her.

Her face was open, expectant.

I had to get over my embarrassment, for Charlie's sake. I didn't want him to become a victim of my lack of self-control. "Sure. I'll pick you up." I opened the door and turned to face her again. "Thanks for the bed." And then I was gone.

Chapter Six

When I got home, I did the things a person does when they have spent the night away, like showering. And all the time I was doing these normal things, I agonised over my actions at Emily's. Had I imagined our mutual attraction? Did I push too hard, take too strong a lead, expect gratification from someone who wasn't interested in me that way? No. Emily had wanted me as much as I wanted her, of that, I was sure. The main thing still bugging me was the way she had said she didn't want to be another notch, another one night stand. What on earth had she meant by that? I did not sleep around. I had never slept around. What had made her think I did?

I rummaged inside my jacket pocket and pulled out my mobile phone. Should I call and ask her? Right. That plan was out of the window, as there was no way I would be doing that. What about Abbie? Fuck no. I would have to admit that I'd got jiggy with it, or tried to, with Lily's new best friend.

I slipped the phone back into my pocket and then went out to my truck. It was half past ten, and I needed to pick Emily up to go and visit Charlie. I had no doubt it was going to be an interesting day.

She was waiting at the gate for me as I pulled up. Her face looked pale, and the smile she gave me was hesitant. I would like to say that I felt no physical attraction for her, but that would make me a liar. I felt more than a physical attraction for her; that was why I was finding the situation so difficult.

"Hey. You're early," Emily said.

I wanted to carry on with our joke about her already waiting for me, but instead I smiled and patted the seat next to me.

The journey to the Trust was quiet, with few remarks. When we arrived, Charlie was waiting for us, his tail banging on the floor and his ball wedged in his mouth. A mewling noise slipped around the plastic orb. and I felt the first spurt of happiness I'd felt all day.

"Hello there, fella."

More mewling and tail thumping.

Emily crouched beside me and tickled Charlie's ears. He was like putty in her hands. She laughed and then looked at me, her face beaming. "Looks like someone is happy to see us."

I nodded.

"Shall we let him off the lead today?"

My grin slipped. More risk? Look what had happened last night when I had decided to take a leap of faith.

As if Emily had read my mind, she placed her hand on my knee and said, "We have to take a chance sooner or later, Ellie. Might as well be now."

Was she talking about Charlie, or me and her?

"He's a good boy, and he loves us. He will come when we

call him, I promise."

To be honest, I didn't want to do it. I had only known him for ten days, and I didn't think that he would respond to me as readily as I felt he needed to. Come to think of it, that also meant I had only known Emily for ten days. So why did it feel as if I had known her all my life?

"Okay."

"Okay?"

"Okay. Let's try him." I watched her face go from glowing to seriously excited. "But..." I grabbed her hand and pulled her to me, "…only for a little while."

"Suits me."

Then she did something I hadn't thought she would ever do again. She drew me close and hugged me hard. I felt a soft kiss on my cheek, and then the coolness of the air as she pulled away and opened the door to Charlie's kennel. What happened in the next few minutes, I can't actually remember.

He was perfect. Absolutely perfect. He raced after his ball, brought it back, saw a squirrel and ignored it; he was too busy showing us what an adorable, well-behaved little man he was. Charlie trotted between Emily and me as if he was trying to balance his affection. Instead of the "little while" off the lead, it ended up with him being off the lead for the majority of our walk. Every time I went to clip the lead back on, Emily said "Just a little while longer" and I was faced by two pairs of brown eyes pleading with me to take a chance. I couldn't resist either set.

Back at the kennels, I felt the all-too-familiar tug inside my chest as I had to say farewell to Charlie. My throat constricted, and I knew that I was about to cry. I hated leaving him there, hated the way he would scamper into his kennel and then turn to sit and look at us with such love. How could he understand that it wasn't our choice to leave him? How could he know that I wanted to take him home with me? But, then again, so did Emily.

As soon as I had clicked my seatbelt into place, Emily said, "We need to talk."

Shit.

"About last night."

Double shit. Shall I go for verbal diarrhoea? I grunted and started the engine.

"Let's get lunch somewhere and talk. Neutral ground."

I grunted again as I released the hand brake.

Emily sigh deeply as she pulled the hand brake back on. "El-lie. We need to clear the air."

"It's clear enough from where I'm sitting." I released the hand brake, just to have her click it back into place. I tried again, but her hand covered mine. "What?" I glared at Emily, who just raised her eyebrow and made her expression appear quite menacing. "I thought you wanted to get lunch. How can we get lunch if you won't let me fucking drive there?"

Yes. I know. I shouldn't have snapped and I shouldn't have sworn, but...what I said was actually right, wasn't it?

I expected her to look hurt, you know, do the female thing of slumping in her seat and having a face on her that could put a damper on any occasion, but no.

She was leaning forward, her top lip snarling and a hint of

murder in the once soft brown eyes. "Well *fucking* drive, then."

Her words weren't spoken, they were growled, and strangely enough, that sent a tingle down my spine.

As soon as I pulled to a stop in a parking spot, she shot out of the car, slammed the door behind her, and marched off into the pub.

With a shrug, I pulled on my hand brake and took a deep breath before following her. Part of me was not looking forward to our "needing to talk," and still, it wouldn't hurt to clear the air—as in, have a good old fashioned argument. At least a shouting match would relieve some of the built up sexual tension I was still harbouring from the previous evening.

I readily spotted Emily when I entered. She'd claimed a seat in the corner, away from prying eyes and, hopefully, bat-like ears.

Instead of going over to her, I went to the bar and got us drinks and picked up a menu that boasted "The Best Carvery in Town." How original. And how trite was I being? I turned back to Emily, who was glaring at me from her remoteness. "You want a carvery?" I mouthed.

Her glare didn't change. I took that as a "yes."

I gave her the thumbs up before ordering two carveries from the barman, who seemed as if he would have been more at home doing his homework or updating his profile on Facebook.

"Done." I plonked the drinks down and the slips we had to present to get our food. "Want to eat before you rip my head off ? I'd hate for you to get filled up by chewing my ass off."

Emily opened her mouth to retort, but closed it again.

I slipped onto the bench seat and moved next to her.

"I'm sorry, Ellie."

What for? Leading me on or being aggressive?

"I've been totally out of order."

I pursed my lips and nodded agreeably.

"I just...well, I like you."

Huh? She liked me? God only knew how she would be acting if she loved me. I would probably be in Accident and Emergency by now, or six feet under.

"If you like me, why did last night happen?" Listen to me and my ability to get right to the point. I think that was a first.

"It happened because I do like you." Emily grabbed her drink and took a gulp.

"You leading me on, letting me...you know...and then treating me as a mistake you couldn't wait to get rid of?" God, I felt in control. That didn't happen often, and I wanted to revel in the sensation. Well, not really. In fact I was dying a thousand deaths, I felt so exposed. But I had to know, had to find out why.

"I didn't want to be a statistic."

"A fucking what?" That came out a little bit louder than I had intended. I lowered my voice, even though half the patrons in the pub were now looking in our direction. Even the teen behind the bar had stopped Tweeting. "A fucking statistic? What the hell do you mean by that?"

She gritted her teeth together before she took another swallow of her drink. I was happy I'd only gotten her a Coke, otherwise, at this rate she would soon be too pissed to talk.

"Michelle told me about your phone call."

Phone call?

"The woman you were apologising to."

Apologising?

"And when I asked you if you had anyone special, you said

no."

"But there isn't anyone special." I watched the sadness cloud her face, and then pass as if I had dreamed it.

"That's obvious."

"I have no idea what you are talking about. If you didn't want to—"

"Too right I don't want to. I don't want to be with someone who sleeps with one woman one night, and is then trying to get into another's bed the next."

Something was ringing in my head—a memory, a realization, an epiphany. She was talking about my fake call to my sister, the same sister I would have sworn would tell Emily what I had done. At that critical moment, I did something stupid. I started laughing.

Important tip! Don't laugh at a woman who wants to shove her fist down your throat to start with. It only pisses her off even more.

"So I'm a laughingstock now, am I?"

Fuck. She looked so mad, it made me laugh even harder.

"Right. That's it." Emily bolted to her feet, tipping the table as she did so.

My drink wobbled precariously, and I tried to stop it. Instead, I knocked it towards her, and it spilled all over her jeans.

"Jesus! Fuck me." Not the right thing to shout out in a public house at Sunday lunchtime.

"Sorry. I'm sorry." I tried to wipe her off, but I only had my hands and they weren't doing a very good job.

Emily grabbed one of my hands and peeled it off of her. "Save it for one of your conquests, Anderson."

"For fuck's sake!" I stood up and leaned towards her in fury.

"Including nearly sleeping with you last night, I haven't had sex with a woman in nearly two years!"

Tink.

If you are wondering what the "tink" was, it was the sound of a pin dropping somewhere in the pub.

"Everyone is staring, aren't they?" My voice was barely audible; pity it hadn't been that way on the previous tidbit of information I had decided to share.

Emily's eyes darted past me, and she nodded. "Nearly everyone. The old bloke reading the paper isn't... Oh, wait, now he's looking."

I slowly sat down at the table and rummaged around in my pockets. "Here." I held out a couple of tissues for her to mop some of the Coke from her jeans.

"Thank you."

My. Weren't we being civilised.

Sounds started to filter back through the pub, and I just knew that most of the voices were discussing my admission. Although lesbianism was somewhat acceptable and more common in 2012, people still found it a riveting topic of conversation.

As I wiped the table with the last of my tissues, Emily stilled my hand. When I looked up at her, my gaze was met by understanding brown eyes.

"For the record, I haven't had sex in nearly three years." She barked a rueful laugh. "And that was the night before I found out she was sleeping with everyone else."

"Shit."

"By the bucket."

There was an awkward silence brought on by each of us feeling exposed. I looked around for some inspiration for conversation. "I think our carvery tickets are a bit wet." I held up the soggy pieces of paper and grinned at her, and I was rewarded with a truly wonderful smile in return. God bless food tickets.

"You ready for 'The Best Carvery in Town'?"

She nodded, a comical smile on her face. "Lay on, MacDuff."

So I did.

Conversation over lunch was more relaxed. We actually spoke to each other instead of trying to rip each other's head off. I wanted to ask Emily more about the woman who had cheated on her, but I didn't think it was appropriate for me to ask. I would wait until she wanted to talk about it. That was the thing to do after all—show my sensitive side.

"Ellie? Can I ask you something?" The tone of her voice gave away the fact that what she wanted to ask me wouldn't be good for me. "Who was on the phone yesterday morning when you were talking to Michelle?"

Told you.

"Abbie."

I watched her face twist into a look of horror, and I realised she must be thinking I was doing unnatural things with my sister. It was time to confess.

"I assumed Michelle was your girlfriend and...and I didn't want to seem so...so..."

"Single?"

"Single" sounded better than "desperate," which is what I was going to say, so I nodded. "Yes. Single." Desperate actually was more honest. "Also, I didn't want Michelle to think I had tickets on her girl."

A soft smile lit Emily's face. "But I told you about Tania. What did you... No! You didn't think I was in a relationship with someone who would sleep with someone else and tell me about it, did you?"

Once again, I nodded.

"Bugger." Then she laughed. "Wait until I tell Michelle. She will pee her pants."

My look of mortification was easy to read, and she laughed again. "No worries. I'll keep mum."

After we had finished eating, I drove her home with the promise to be at her place bright and early the next day. It would be the beginning of a new week, hopefully a new chapter, in my life. This time without crossed wires and lack of communication.

I could hope, couldn't I?

Chapter Seven

Nearly a week had passed since the episode in the pub, and nothing was ever mentioned about it again. We still went to see Charlie every day and then went back to Emily's for lunch before we each got on with our own work for the rest of the day. I found myself daydreaming a little too frequently to actually get a spark on and finish the jobs on Emily's garden that I set out for myself each day. There were way too many times I came around from some mind fart with my head resting on the handle of my spade. Oddly enough, it always seemed that when that happened, Emily was doing something in front of me. If she ever saw me spacing out, she never said anything about it.

I wanted to bring up things. And when I say "things," I mean things like asking her out on a date. But since the fiasco of the previous week, she had not given any indication that she wanted to pursue anything further. She knew I wasn't a Lady Killer—far from it—unless you can bore someone to death by talking about plants and dogs, then I am guilty as charged. We each knew the other was single, were attracted to each other, had nearly made the beast with two backs six days ago and thoroughly enjoyed it—at least I did, until I realised I was on my own in that experience, although now I knew why the fire had been dampened for her. So why nothing since?

Although I wanted her—God, I wanted her—I don't think I was ready for anything to happen. That's my excuse for not bringing it up, although I wanted to bring "things" up. Jesus Christ. I'm confused, so God only knows how you feel.

Maybe it was Charlie. No. I don't mean that he pulled me to one side and said in his best kindly doggy way, "Don't bother asking her out. She'll shoot you down." It was more that if I allowed myself to become attached to Emily, to date her, then what would happen when the month was up and we had to decide who Charlie was going to live with? Could I let myself become all loved up and then say, "No. Charlie is my dog. Fuck off." I doubted it.

So, here I was digging a hole for a fence post—one of many in my life, both literal and metaphorical—and daydreaming about asking out a woman I would never ask out.

Yep. I'm an idiot.

A few days later, I went to see Abbie. Lily was concerned about me arriving on my own and not having Emily with me, so she didn't give me the time of day. She decided to play with her pooch instead. Poppy was well-established in their household by now and had everyone in the palm of her paw. For some reason, I was feeling a little over-sensitive. I wanted to cry, drop to my knees and holler, "My beloved family. Come to me." At one point I had to mentally count the days until my period to make sure I wasn't ovulating.

After cadging a cuppa, I suggested taking Poppy for a walk, and Lily shouted for Jessie J. I had to grin inwardly, not because she had named the dog after the singer, but because the pup completely disregarded being called by that name by running in the opposite direction.

"Watch this, Aunty Wellie." Lily unclipped the lead from Poppy. "Sit."

Poppy sat.

"Staaaaaaaaay."

The dog stayed as Lily backed away from her. "Sta-aaaaaaaaaaaaay."

Poppy looked expectant.

"Come here, Jessie!" Lily slapped her hands on her thighs; the pooch stood up, but then sat back down.

"Jessie!"

Except for a slight twitch, the dog stayed.

"Try using her name."

"I am."

"Her real name."

Lily tutted and stared hard at Poppy as if she was sending a message telepathically. Lily sighed. "Poppy!"

The little Jack Russell ran over and jumped up to lick Lily's hands, which were now waving excitedly in the air.

I clapped and cheered, telling Lily how clever she was for teaching Poppy so well.

The little mite just glared at me before cuddling Poppy to her. "I didn't. She came like this."

What was she? A new gadget? Where are the instructions?

I grinned at Lily. "But she wouldn't do her tricks for just anyone, now would she?"

Lily became even more excited, and proceeded to tell Poppy

to sit and stay about forty times.

By the time we got back to the house, Poppy and Lily were beat and decided "they both" needed to watch TV. Rob was at work, so that gave Abbie and me a chance to have a catch up session in the kitchen.

"What's up?"

I don't know how my sister does that. She wasn't even looking at me at the time.

"Why should anything be up?"

Abbie snorted as she continued to brew the tea.

"Why're you snorting?"

She snorted again.

"There's nothing up. What makes you say that?" Was I being too insistent? Was that the reason she could read me like a book? "Abbie?"

"For fuck's sake, Elles, I was just inquiring how you are. But by the sounds of it," she turned with the mugs in her hand and sporting a huge grin, "I think you need to talk to your older, and very understanding sister." The mugs hit the table. "Spill."

"There's nothing to spill." I pulled the drink over to me and held onto it as if it could shield me from my sister's powers of perception.

Abbie snorted again.

"Have you got a cold?" I asked.

Abbie disregarded the comment and looked me squarely in the eyes. "Look, sis, no offence, but when was the last time you came to see me in the middle of a work day?"

I stared at her blankly.

"I'll tell you when—when you lost Toby five years ago."

That couldn't be right. I came to visit all the time.

"Don't get me wrong, you come to see us."

See.

"Just not when you should be working." Abbie leaned over and took the cup from my hands and placed it on the table. "So, you can see why I am a little concerned."

I didn't say anything.

"How's Charlie?"

"Good. Great. Actually, more than great."

"How's the arrangement between you and Emily padding out?"

"What do you mean by that?" How could she get me to expose my thoughts so easily?

"I actually meant about you going to see Charlie together, but I think maybe..." She cocked her head to the side and one eyebrow raised. "You've fallen for her, haven't you?"

I made a pfffft sound and reached for my drink, but she moved it away from my grasp.

"You have! You've fallen for the gorgeous Ms Carson!"

Abbie threw her head back and laughed out loud—or loled, as modern language dictates we say. At least it was better than her snorting, although not by much.

"No I haven't!"

"Ellie fancies Emily!"

"No I don't!" Even I didn't believe me.

"You like Aunty Ems?" Lily had appeared just in time to witness my transformation from human to beetroot. "You gunna marry her?"

Poppy skidded around my niece and hopped up onto my knee and stared intently into my eyes.

Somewhere in the background I heard the doorbell chime, but was too mortified to move.

Abbie was pointing at me and laughing, just like she used

to do when we were kids. And just like when we were kids, I hated it.

I could hear Lily talking to someone and telling them her Aunty Wellie was going to marry Emily, and then I realised Abbie had suddenly stopped laughing. I saw the colour drain from Abbie's face, and I didn't get why. It seemed as if everything had slowed down, like when a video tape is showing each screen shot.

"What?"

My face took an age to turn from my sister's ashen appearance to the reappearance of Lily coming through the doorway, her mouth still moving but the words seemingly unintelligible. She was holding a hand. An older hand. She was totally animated, in slow motion. Her face turned towards me, and I could see the happiness beaming there. Lily nodded in my direction, and then looked up again. My eyes followed the trajectory of her gaze, and I came eye to eye with my mother.

Thirteen years.

That was how long it had been since I had last looked into her eyes. I wish I could say the expression was softer, the eyes more understanding, the hatred gone. But I can't. The look she gave me clearly showed me that it didn't matter how much time passed, she would never forgive me for being who I was and not what she expected me to be.

It still hurt. Fuck. More than hurt. Although I had spent the last thirteen years not expecting a hearts and flowers reunion, it was like a kick in the gut to know that it wouldn't matter if it was thirty years; I would still not be accepted for being me.

"Mum? What're you doing here?"

I could hear panic in Abbie's voice. I knew she still saw our parents, my mother didn't have a grievance with the ones who conformed to her idea of propriety, but it was still a shock to see her in my sister's kitchen, holding hands with my niece.

"Aunty Wellie is g'ttin' married to Emily."

No, Lily. Not now.

"No, Lily. A woman can't marry another woman."

Yes they can.

"It's unnatural."

No, it isn't. Love is love. And if I wanted to marry Emily Carson, I bloody well would.

"I should go."

"Ellie!" My sister's voice was pleading. "Don't. Stay."

"I'll speak to you later, sis."

I was amazed that I could say anything, considering the size of the lump in my throat. Abbie opened her mouth to say something else, but I leaned over and kissed her cheek. I ruffled Lily's hair. "I'll come again at the weekend."

She let go of her grandmother's hand and clung to my leg. "Stay. Poppy needs you." Her grip was constricting. "Me needs you too."

I tried to peel her off me, but she wasn't having any of it, so I had to shuffle away from the scene in the kitchen with my niece hanging on to my leg for dear life. Not the way I envisioned exiting the unexpected meeting with my mother, but what else could I do?

Thankfully, Abbie came to my rescue. She followed me outside and lifted Lily off me. Green eyes looked concerned as I climbed into my cab.

"I'll call you later, Elles."

I nodded as I started the engine. I knew that two pairs of green eyes were watching me as I drove down the road, and I missed their presence as I turned the corner and went back to the emptiness of the day.

As soon as I got home, I turned off my mobile. It was almost like Auden's poem, but instead of the "Stop all the clocks, cut off the telephone, Prevent the dog from barking with a juicy bone," it seemed more like "I thought that love would last forever; I was wrong." Too fucking right. Love doesn't last forever. And it hurt to know that for certain. Love was a bitch.

How could my own parents turn their backs on me just because I never wanted to be with a man? Had I hurt anyone? Apparently. Them, by their account. It didn't matter that I had done everything they had ever wanted, apart from conform to the romantic "norm." I hadn't been a wild teenager, never gave them reason to ground me. I wasn't experimenting with lads behind the bike sheds or in the back seat of a crappy car. Maybe I should've, then I would have been more what they wanted. Would they have been happier if I had come home pregnant, or run away with some spotty teenager who happened to have a dick?

Where had my philosophical, "Too much has happened in my life to worry about their insensitivity and inability to love me no matter what" gone to? What had happened in between, what had happened before—it didn't really matter, did it? I am gay. I prefer the company of women, although I hadn't actually been with a woman for so long, I was more asexual than lesbian.

The image of my mother's face popped into my mind. It had been thirteen years since I had seen her. I was hoping that her turning her back on me would have aged her, would have eaten her up with guilt, but no. She looked just the same as she always had, maybe a little older, but nothing of note. Part of me wondered what my father looked like, but then I thought "Who gives a shit?" I also wondered if they were happy that they had cut me out of their lives. Probably. And once again, "Who gives a shit?" It was obvious they didn't care whether or not I was happy. They would have preferred that I pretend I was something that I wasn't, that I live a life of misery rather than accept who I was.

Fuck 'em.

Twats.

Fucking twats.

I'd moved from hurt to anger in the space of thirty minutes. And with anger comes more anger.

How dare they? How fucking dare they try to mess up my life after all this time? Wasn't it bad enough they had kicked me out when I was twenty with no means of looking after myself? They'd totally expected me to recant my claim on a life of degradation and come scuttling home with my and Toby's tail between our respective legs.

Obviously, we hadn't.

My lips peeled back from my teeth in a menacing grin. I bet my refusal to conform fucked them off big time. Images of my childhood rattled through my head. All the times my mother reprimanded me for just being a kid. Times when I wanted to share something with her, and she dismissed me with a look or a wave of her hand. School productions were never attended. Parents' Evening was always met with "So, she could do better?" never a "Well done for coming top in English," just a sneer and "You should work harder at Maths and Science. They're more important."

Don't get me wrong, all my childhood wasn't so bad. I had Abbie. It constantly surprises me how normal she turned out to be. She never let them get to her...never let them win. No wonder she got married so young. Yes, she loves Rob, but maybe getting married so young wasn't just because they couldn't wait to get hitched. I wondered what her story was. Had my parents tried to intervene with her life like they had mine?

"Brrrrrrrrrrriiiiiiiiiiiiiiiiiiiiiiiiiiiiiiiiiiiiiiiinnnnnnnnnnnnnnnn nnnngggggggg!"

The sound of my house phone nearly made me pee myself. I lunged towards it, but stopped before lifting it from its cradle.

Click. I listened to my voice announce that I couldn't get to the phone right now, but if they would like to leave a message...

"Hey, Ellie."

Why was Emily calling me? I'd seen her that morning. Walked Charlie with her, told her I was visiting my sister because the supplies I needed to finish the back fencing weren't in yet.

"I...um...how're you?"

Huh?

"I tried your mobile, but it went straight to answer phone. Can you call me back when you get this?"

I could, but that didn't mean I would.

"Or Abbie."

Bingo.

"Okay. Speak soon."

Abbie had called her. I knew it in my bones. I bet if I turned on my mobile, it would have a missed call, maybe a couple of messages from my sister. I was surprised she had waited as long as she had. How long had it been since I had left her? An hour? Where was the witch whilst Abbie was calling me? Stirring her cauldron?

Stop. Why was I having a go at Abbie? It wasn't her fault

she was straight and had kept in contact with our parents. I was becoming bitter—or had I always been bitter and this was just an outburst, a bit like herpes?

I lifted the phone and dialed. It only rang a couple of times before a very familiar voice answered.

"Hey. You busy? Fancy meeting up for a bit?"

I was on the phone for less than a minute, and I felt better already. I had to get myself into gear, as I now had plans. I decided on a quick shower and a fresh set of clothes. Couldn't be going to a pub at six in my work gear, could I? And I didn't think Abbie would be too happy if I turned up stinking of toil, sweat, and tears.

Obviously I didn't call Emily. I needed to speak to my sister; that was why I had gone around to see her in the first place.

Glancing through the window as I moved towards the bathroom, I felt a twinge of guilt when I spotted the supplies for the back fence under the tarpaulin sheeting where I had hidden them. I half-smiled. At least I'd fooled one person today. Fooling my sister was a completely different kettle of fish. She could spot a cover up before a person had time to blink.

Abbie was already at the pub when I arrived. Apparently she had left Lily at home with Rob. She was probably driving him mad with dog tricks and sing-alongs.

As soon as Abbie saw me, she stood and rushed towards me, then scooped me into her arms and hugged me close. "Sorry about earlier."

I shrugged and tried to pull away.

"No. I am. I should've put Mum in her place."

I tried to pull away again. "People are looking. They'll think we're a couple."

"Let them look. When they're talking about us, they are leaving some other poor bastard alone."

I laughed and tilted my head back to look at her.

Abbie had one raised eyebrow and a self-satisfied smirk. "Fancy something to eat? This place boasts the best carvery in town."

Bollocks. I'd forgotten about that when we had made the arrangements. I laughed, and Abbie looked at me questioningly.

"Nothing. Sit. I'll be hunter gatherer."

I wasn't surprised to see the same barman waiting for me. He gave me a knowing nod and a wink before asking what he could get for me. Cheeky bastard. Couldn't he see Abbie and me were related? I shrugged it aside and gave him my order.

As he passed me my change, he leaned in conspiratorially and whispered, "I won't say a word."

I glared in response. What a wanker.

Abbie waited until we had eaten before she brought up the subject of our parents.

Instead of answering her question about how I was feeling, I dived in with, "Why did you marry Rob so young?"

She cocked her head and looked at me with confusion. "Because we love each other."

"I know that, but why so young? Why didn't you just live together first?"

Abbie laughed. "Do I really have to explain that to you?"

No. She didn't. She hadn't been allowed to just "live" with the man she loved; she had to conform to parental expectations. But that wasn't the Abbie that I knew. My Abbie would've told Mum to fuck off and moved in with Rob anyway.

I didn't have to ask her again. She sighed and pushed her empty plate away. "It was made clear that if I lived "in sin" with Rob, I would no longer be welcome at home."

I shrugged. To me that would have been no big loss.

"And that would've meant I wouldn't get to see you. Mum made it very clear that I would be a bad influence on you."

"But I was old enough to come and see you...old enough to make my own choices."

Abbie leaned over and grabbed my hand, and I could feel the barman's eyes on us. Pervert.

"It doesn't matter, does it? It is all in the past. Rob and I love each other and would've got married sooner or later."

"But—"

"No buts, Elles. It is what it is. I'm happy." She stared into my eyes intently. "Are you?"

I looked at her in confusion.

"Happy?"

I opened my mouth, but couldn't decide whether to say yes or no.

"You could be, if you gave her a chance."

"I did. I have. We did...erm...nothing."

"What the fuck? You did...erm...nothing? Story of your life, little sis."

I bit my top lip to stifle my initial retort, giving a very good impression of a bulldog in the process. "We nearly...then we didn't. She... I... Bollocks."

"Have you asked her out on a date? A proper date and not 'Let's go and see Charlie'?"

I was sure I had. Sure of it. Near the beginning—

The lunch, yes. No. It was just lunch after all. Rob's Bash! No, once again. I had to be told to go and pick her up, which is something you don't normally do when on a date.

I opened my mouth to answer, and then this wonderful image of a certain brown-eyed boy appeared in front of my eyes. Charlie. He was the reason I hadn't asked Emily out on a date. And why did I have to go through all the different scenarios before I was reminded of the reason why I hadn't formally asked Emily Carson out? I shook my head to dispel the thought, but Abbie took it as negation.

"You need to—"

"No I don't." I whipped my hand from hers.

"Yes. You do." She grabbed my hand back and dragged me over the top of the table, not right over, but far enough for us to be eye to eye.

I looked over her shoulder and saw the barman giving me the thumbs up. I wanted to send him the British two fingered salute, but I couldn't get my other hand around to make it as effective as I wanted.

"I'm really proud of you for putting your heart out there again with Charlie, but you need a woman in your life."

That was the problem though, wasn't it? I couldn't have one without losing the other. If I allowed Emily into my life, Charlie would be hers, or else it would be a case of what I said before— if I tried to keep Charlie for myself, where would that leave Emily and me?

Suddenly it was as if a light clicked on inside my head. Not a very bright light, but a light all the same. But wouldn't I lose her friendship, too? I hadn't thought of that before. All I had focused on was us having a relationship not a friendship. But I didn't want to lose her friendship. I'd just found it. Just found her. Why did I have to choose? Why couldn't I have both?

"You know, if you and Emily did get together, then maybe

both of you could have Charlie."

I heard the words coming from Abbie's mouth, but found it difficult to process them. How could we both have Charlie? I would be at my house, and she would be at hers. I wanted Charlie full time. A little voice squeaked inside my chest, "And you want Emily full time, too."

"My head hurts. Can't we just—"

"No. You need to talk about it, Ellie. You can't keep crawling back under your anti-relationship rock. I know you've been hurt. I know losing Toby was tough...and losing Mum and Dad."

"I don't give a shit about those two." Abbie didn't comment, as it was obvious I did care.

"You need to let Emily in. If it is just sex, then it's just sex, but you have to start living again, baby."

"You ladies finished?" The barman had decided Facebook wasn't as interesting as the two women in the corner, and he had come to clear our table. "Can I do anything else for you?"

I really wanted to say, "Yeah. Fuck off," but I'm too much of a lady.

"Would you like...some dessert?"

I just glared at him until he departed.

"I want a sundae with nuts," Abbie said, whilst trying to conjure an expression of fake sadness, like her world would be crushed if she didn't get her dessert.

Huh? How did we go from talking about sex to sundaes?

"And chocolate sauce." Abbie let go of my hand and stood. "I'll be the hunter this time. You just sit and think."

I didn't. I sat and fiddled. I sat and shuffled. I sat and leaned on and off the table until Abbie returned.

"I'm on a diet," she announced.

"And?"

"A little of what you fancy makes the whole world better." Abbie sipped her Diet Coke and looked smug. "Why deprive yourself of life's little pleasures when indulging now and again makes everything slot back into place."

What was she talking about?

"I ordered yours without nuts."

"Why? You know I love nuts."

"Because you are a lesbian, and lesbians don't eat nuts."

Of course she said that just at the time the ice cream arrived, much to the delight of the barman, who was undoubtedly now going to be our waiter for the evening.

Both sundaes were covered in nuts.

"Gotcha." She picked up her spoon. "See? You can have both—ice cream and nuts."

I just shook my head and gave her a look of sympathy. "You're nuts."

"Eat. Or I will be forced to eat it for you."

So I did.

Chapter Eight

I couldn't sleep properly. Every time I closed my eyes, I saw images of things I didn't want to remember. Why is it when you can't sleep, you can never think of all the good stuff in your life? But then again, what good stuff?

Abbie. Lily. Rob, on occasion. Joking. Charlie. And... Emily. But the last two could so easily fail to become the "good stuff" in my life. They could so easily become the stuff that I packed away and hid at the back of my wardrobe to collect dust and if-onlys.

I watched dawn break and lay there for a little while longer before dragging my ass out of bed. I had work to do at Emily's, and then we would be off to the kennels to see Charlie before lunch. It was only a week before the decision about who was going to have him, and I was half excited and half shitting my pants. But at least I would soon know, one way or the other. Unfortunately. Or fortunately. Or back again to unfortunately. I could go on, but I think you've got the gist of it.

By the time I arrived, Emily was already outside and trimming down a door. I sat in the truck and watched her with riveted fascination as she guided the jigsaw through the wood, her goggles firmly in place, her ponytail bobbing with her effort. Once again I was blown away by her. Why did she have to be so beautiful? So wonderful? So...so...Emily.

"Morning, you!"

In my cloud of longing, I hadn't even noticed the jigsaw being shut down. Emily had pushed the goggles up and was grinning at me whilst waving the power tool in the air.

"Did you get the supplies for the back fence?"

Yes. But they were still in my back garden covered by a tarpaulin.

I grinned the grin of a woman who was trying her damnedest to cover her lie. "I've got to pick it up in a little while."

Emily set the jigsaw down and came over to me.

"Shouldn't take me long to collect it from B&Q."

"Great! Can I cadge a lift? I've got to pick up some supplies myself, and it would save time if we went together."

Shiiiiiiiiiiit. "I could get them for you. Save even more time." I could hear the pleading tone in my voice; it was a pity she couldn't.

"Don't worry about me."

I opened my mouth to spew out another pile of shite, but she continued, "Then we could go straight to see Charlie. It's on the way."

True. But that didn't change the fact I had lied to her the previous day, did it?

"Want a cuppa?"

She didn't even wait for my response. She was on her way to the house before I could form the words "Fucking hell." Excuse the slip into rude vernacular, although I believe you already knew I tend to swear quite readily.

It was the galvanised nails scenario all over again, but this time the shoe was on the other foot—actually on the other foot of the other person, that person being me. Emily had once changed our time slot and pretended it was because she had to collect a special delivery. Her lie was a little more acceptable, though. She had done so because she had wanted to invite me to lunch. I, on the other hand, had lied so I could run babbling to my big sister about why I couldn't sort my life out into clear cut categories. At least I got ice cream.

I dragged my feet on my way to the house. If I walked slowly, maybe I could think up an excuse before I got there. Unfortunately, the thinking part of my brain was elsewhere—probably at a party with other parts of my brain, discussing what a knob I am over cocktails and sausages on sticks. If I'd been invited, I would have agreed with my brain's assessment.

Looking towards the house, I could see Emily at the window watching me. Her hands were resting on the sill, and she was staring intently in my direction.

A butterfly took off somewhere in the region of my gut and started to tippy-toe its way through my insides. I saw her body straighten and turn away quickly, as if she didn't want me to see her. A grin split my face. "Too late, lady." For a split second I felt in control, until I remembered that I was still a back fence hiding twat.

All the way to B&Q, I tried to think of excuses, but I came up with nothing. Emily was checking her list and rattling on about hoping everything was ready so she didn't have to keep me waiting. I was beginning to pale. Why hadn't I just answered her with "Oh yeah. I picked them up yesterday and took them home. That's why I missed your call." Because, as my brain cells had all agreed, I am a knob.

As we got out of the truck, I turned to Emily and said, "I'll be over at Trade. Shall we meet back here?"

She shook her head and smiled that adorable smile of hers. "I'm going to Trade, too."

Shhhhhhiiit.

"Oh, wait. I need to go and check out the flooring tiles," she said.

Thank you, God!

"Meet you in a few."

I raced over to the trade counter and had to wait behind a bloke who thought displaying the crack of his arse to everyone in the vicinity was standard behaviour and perfectly acceptable. In my head I was repeating the mantra "hurry up," before I realised I didn't actually have to queue, as I had nothing to collect. I stepped back, turned, and started away from the counter.

"There you are. Finished already?"

I nodded enthusiastically.

Emily looked behind me and pulled a face. "So...where is the fencing?"

I laughed, a little bit hysterically if you ask me, and shook my head. "You won't believe this." Because it's a lie. "They've delivered it to my place already."

Emily cocked her head, her brow furrowed. "Really?"

I nodded again.

"Do they do that without you asking?'"

I opened my mouth to tell more lies, but was stopped by the voice of the builder behind me.

"Sorry about keeping you waiting, love. These lot couldn't find their dicks with both hands." And then he scuttled off, hoisting his jeans to crack height as he went.

"Pfft. I've always found them to be efficient." Was my voice always that high? By the amused look on Emily's face, I took that as a "no."

"Do you need me to help you collect your stuff?"

Emily grinned that half grin of hers before shaking her head.

"Okay. I'll meet you at the truck." I was almost running as I left her, but I still heard her laughing as I went.

Fifteen minutes later, Emily appeared with a trolley full of supplies. Well, I say she appeared with it, but that isn't quite right. She was being helped by a very attractive young woman who was wearing the B&Q uniform.

A spark of jealousy shot through me, and I jumped out of the cab and took over the pushing of the trolley. "Here, let me." It is amazing I didn't cock my leg and piss all over her.

Emily nodded and smiled, then turned back to the woman to continue their conversation while I ended up loading the truck on my own. With each item, the thudding as it hit the inside of my truck became louder. But neither of them gave any indication that they were listening.

"Okay, Cathy. Lovely to see you again."

I gritted my teeth.

"We'll get together soon, yes?"

My jaw cracked with the pressure of my grimace.

"Hey. You've loaded it all. Aren't you a star?"

I opened my mouth to answer, but Emily turned to wave at the retreating blonde. "She's such a lovely girl."

I mouthed the same and mimed sticking my fingers down my throat.

"Bye, Cathy!"

I did the same thing again. Funnily enough, it didn't surprise me how petty and childish I could become. Actually, I enjoyed it.

"All set?" Emily looked animated. "Back to yours?"

Huh?

"To get the back fence."

"Oh, yeah. The back fence," I mumbled.

Emily grinned knowingly.

It wasn't until I had collected the fence from my garden, much to the amusement of Ms Carson, that the topic of Cathy was brought up. Like vomit. Why did Emily find it necessary to list the positive qualities about the bimbo at B&Q? Just because she had qualifications growing out of her arse, a fantastic eye for property development, and was knockout gorgeous didn't mean Cathy had it all. She worked at B&Q. B AND Q. And she wasn't so fucking gorgeous, truth be told. I'd seen better, although I wasn't quite so bitter about it then.

It was when Emily said why "Cathy the Perfect One" worked at B&Q, that I rejoined the conversation. Her husband was the manager of the timber department. Cathy was helping him out. Did you get that? Hus-band. Hus-b-and. And this husband was a friend of Emily's from years back, as he'd worked for her on occasion. Yes. Little Miss Fancy Prancy Total Knockout was a Breeder, not a lezza like me. I felt some sense of control returning.

"Why did you lie to me about the fence?"

And…there went the sense of control. Maybe the previous thought was a classic case of pride going before a fall.

"And why didn't you return my call last night?"

Double whammy. What could I tell her? "Oh, sorry, Emily, I was having a relationship crisis and rediscovered my mother hates me more than ever."

"Was it the visit from your mum?"

Bloody Abbie. She'd better not have said anything else.

"I heard you went for another carvery."

This wasn't panning out the way I wanted it to. "Sorry. I... well, I was upset." Might as well be honest. "I'd rather not talk about it, if you don't mind." Just because I was feeling honest, didn't mean I had to tell her anything. My philosophy in life—if you can, keep your mouth shut.

Twenty minutes later, we were with the ball of fluff himself. I watched him with Emily. They looked good together—playing, chasing each other, chasing the ball. I felt tearful for some reason and had to pretend I had a bit of dust in my eye to cover myself.

It didn't seem two minutes until we were back in the truck and on our way back to Emily's. Time with Charlie seemed to get shorter and shorter, although we were there for exactly the same time as usual. It seemed as if the closer D-Day came, the more quickly time was moving. It was usually the other way around, but not on this occasion. I should've been looking forward to the Day of Decision, but I wasn't. The only upside was that Charlie wouldn't have to climb back into his cage and be left again. He would either have the run of Emily's house or mine.

For the rest of the day I kept catching myself looking over at Emily, well, more like daydreaming. Every time I looked at her, I felt a deep yearning. It wasn't sexual; it was so much more. It was as if I needed to be near her, needed to touch her in some capacity to feel right. I was getting the same about leaving her at night as I was when I left Charlie. The only difference was that she knew why I was leaving, and Charlie didn't. That didn't stop me from aching for her.

I felt myself moving towards her on more than one occasion, the words, "Would you come on a date with me?" balancing on the tip of my tongue. I wanted to be with her, see where this could take us. I wanted what we'd had after Rob's party and more...so much more. I wanted the picket fence and the fish pond life, and I wanted them with Emily Carson.

You may have gathered, I didn't ask Emily for a date that day. Or the next day, or the day after that. It actually happened the night before we were to collect Charlie from the Trust, the night before we were going to decide who he would be living with when we picked him up in the morning. Initially, the suggestion was going to be me asking her to come out for a meal so that we could discuss what was going to happen, but when it came down to it, it all changed.

I'd finished making her garden secure—the thing she had employed me to do from the outset. I could've finished it a few days previous, but I kept on dragging things out just so I could spend more time with her. I didn't want to stop going to her house every day, and it wasn't because I enjoyed building fences or levelling her back garden. It was her. Seeing her. Watching her, talking and laughing with her. Each and every day we went to see Charlie, and I felt the pull of both of them, the desire to keep this going for as long as I could.

But it was over. Work was done and Charlie would be with one of us the next day, making the need to see her redundant, making my presence redundant, whether he came home with me or not. I was out of time. I had to make a decision: Walk away and never look back, or push my spine back into place and ask her out on a date.

I would like to say I loaded up my truck, marched into her house, and floored her with my charm. But no. I did load my truck, farted about in the back for an age, scouted around her garden pretending to check if it was safe and then check it all over again, all the time willing myself to ask her out.

"Come on, Anderson. Do it!" I hissed under my breath as I stood dancing from foot to foot at the door of my truck.

The front door to her house opened, and Emily just stood in the doorway and looked at me, a half-smile on her face. Dirt streaked her brow, and some strands of hair had come loose from her ponytail to dance about in the breeze.

"I think I need to pay you, don't you?" she called.

I'd forgotten she still owed me for the work. Shows how love struck I was.

"Come in. Have a coffee and I'll settle up."

This was my moment. This was when the charm would come out, wasn't it? This was when I would ask her, poke out that tongue of mine with the words sitting on the edge. Maybe not. I would just ask her. Ask her. Ask her for a date.

"There you are." She hadn't even looked around, but she knew when I stepped into her kitchen. "Do you want a—"

"Would you like to come out with me tonight?"

"Biscuit?" She stiffened, and I wanted to run. Slowly, too slowly, she turned to look into my eyes. "Why?"

Why? Why? What did she mean by asking why?

"Are you asking me out on a date?"

I couldn't read her expression. It seemed guarded. I wanted to say "to discuss Charlie's future," but that would have been going back on what I'd set out to do. It was shit or bust.

"Erm..." I don't think I'd ever felt so vulnerable. "Would you say 'yes' if I said it was?"

"Yes."

"Because you don't have to say 'yes' if you don't want to."

"Yes."

"Yes?"

"Yes." A smile lit her face as she turned back to making the coffee.

I pumped my fist in the air whilst mouthing "Yes" again. By the time she turned back, I had composed myself. "Go on, then. I'll have a biscuit."

Chapter Nine

I was to pick her up at seven-thirty. The time between me leaving her and me picking her up seemed to last a lifetime. God only knew how I was going to cope with not seeing her on a daily basis.

Unlike every other time I'd arrived at her house, Emily wasn't waiting by the gate. I parked and walked over to her door. It opened just as I got there, and I found I couldn't move. Standing in front of me was a vision. I always knew Emily was beautiful, always knew my heart raced when she was near, or even at the mere thought of her. But at this precise moment, I think my heart actually froze inside my chest. Emily was beauty personified, and I was totally gone.

She was wearing a crisp, white, long sleeved shirt with a glimpse of a pendant around her throat. Her hair was down and wisping around her perfect face. Her lips seemed darker, fuller, even more kissable than they usually did, but it was her eyes that had me. Her eyes, those eyes, the dark brown orbs that seemed to swallow me whole in one glance. I knew I could never tire of looking into those depths, because when I looked into them

I could see my own happiness looking back at me. In that one look, it seemed as if I had been set free from the past, set free from the manacles I'd bound myself with.

"You ready?" I couldn't believe I could actually utter two words.

She nodded and stepped forward, but I was blocking her path. A hint of her scent reached my nostrils, and I moved closer to her as if I was under her spell. I had to tilt my head back so I could keep looking into her eyes. I didn't want to break eye contact, even though I knew I should.

Emily dipped her face to mine, her breath hitting my skin, those eyes becoming even more alluring, mesmerising. It seemed as if she was reading my expression, soaking up my whole being in one look. Closer. It was her or me, or both of us, but we were getting closer, our mouths parting as we closed the distance between us.

The kiss was inevitable, but that still didn't prepare me for how I would feel when those lips touched mine. We had kissed before, but it still came as a wonderful revelation when softness met softness. I felt a click, a lock, a fusion of one soul with another. The kiss was soft, gentle, tender, passionate, and all-consuming. The shock of it raced through my body, claiming every molecule it excited in its passing. Never in my life had I experienced a kiss that made me feel the way her kiss made me feel, and I knew no one else could ever make me feel that way. It was her. Only her. Could only ever be her. My woman. My Emily.

Cold air stung my face as we separated, and I immediately felt the loss of her closeness. Brown eyes widened, as if in realization, and I knew my eyes held the same look.

"I..." She cleared her throat. "I thought I would get that out of the way, or else I would be thinking of kissing you all evening."

I didn't know about her, but I definitely knew I would be thinking about repeating that kiss for the rest of my life.

"Good thinking." Why couldn't I say something as smooth as she had instead of "Good thinking?" Even if I hadn't been a romantic retard in the first place, the kiss would have pushed everything out of my head.

"Shall we?" Emily was still leaning over me, her head tipped as if to kiss me again. She was magnetic, magical, mesmerizing, and I felt the pull of her. Another kiss, comparatively chaste but full of promise. Apart from our lips, we hadn't even touched one another. Our hands had not made contact, although mine kept drifting towards her.

As she drew away, it was a few moments before I could open my eyes and look at her. I wanted to prolong the moment, commit it to memory. I heard her chuckle, and my eyes fluttered open.

"You look adorable."

Adorable? I was going for irresistible.

"Come." Her hand slipped down and captured my own, and she led me to my waiting truck.

All evening, I kept staring at her lips. Well, staring at her lips, her eyes, her hands, and then becoming flustered and talking shite to cover myself. It was amazing to think I had tried to stop from feeling this way about her, but it had been inevitable since the very first moment I met her. I had felt a click, a connection, even when she had me pinned to the floor at the Dogs Trust, but I had pushed away all thoughts of ever being with her because I was too afraid of being rejected or left once again.

Now it was too late for that. It had been too late from the moment I had seen her, seen Charlie. I had let them both in, but believed I couldn't have one without losing the other. That wasn't so. I could have ice cream and nuts, as my sister had said. Although she had coded it to fit with that occasion, she knew I would realise she meant Emily and Charlie. Maybe I couldn't have them with me straight away, but that would come. There would be a place in the near future where I would be with Emily full time and Charlie would be ours—not hers, not mine, ours.

I think I surprised myself by the next thing I said. "I think Charlie should live with you."

Her fork was halfway to her mouth, the food dangling precariously.

"You're his mum."

Clank. The fork hit her plate.

"Elles."

Had she ever called me Elles before? She should have. Her voiced was gentle, reassuring.

"I realised weeks ago that Charlie belongs with you," Emily's voice was so gentle.

"No, I—"

"Yes. He is definitely your boy."

"But—"

"But why did I keep going to see him every day?" A gentle laugh escaped her. "Simple. So I could be with you, be with you both."

My jaw dropped open. To be with me? To be with us both? Apart from the scene on the sofa, had she ever shown me anything beyond friendship? Images flooded my mind of the way she looked at me, the way she spoke to me, the way she cared how I was feeling. Yes. She had. Never had she made me feel less than special, even though I hadn't realised it at the time. I was too busy being a moron.

"Now I feel foolish." She blushed.

"Why foolish?"

She chuckled self-consciously as she fiddled with her napkin. "Because I've just told you I'm falling for you...can't bear to be without you."

Her eyes looked everywhere but at me, so I leaned over and turned her face up with the tips of my fingers. "For the record, I've already fallen."

Her eyes brimmed. She tried to laugh again, but it came out as a half sob. A solitary tear slid down her cheek. I brushed it away, then trailed my thumb over her lip. It was trembling.

Her hand came up and gripped mine. "You don't know how long I've waited to hear you say that."

"And you don't know how long I've wanted to say it."

It was true, even though I hadn't realised it. I felt as if the weight of the world had been lifted from my shoulders, and for the first time in years, I could breathe.

"Dessert?"

We hadn't even noticed the waitress standing next to us, hadn't noticed the table had been cleared.

I smiled at her before nodding at Emily. "I don't know about you, but I want a sundae. With nuts and chocolate sauce."

Her brow furrowed in confusion, but still she grinned.

Must have been the way I'd almost shouted my desire for an ice cream.

The rest of the evening was just as perfect. We discussed her decision to let me take Charlie, and whatever I argued, she refuted. According to her, he belonged with me, and that was the end of it. Anyone overhearing us would have thought that neither of us wanted the little man, but that couldn't have been further from the truth.

On the drive home, I felt the butterflies set up their dance again. Much had happened between us, and I knew the future would be full of things that were just as promising. But the thing uppermost in my mind was what was going to happen when I walked her to her door...the kiss we were going to share before I left her. If it was anything like the kisses we had been sharing all evening, I knew I would be floating home.

When I stopped the car, Emily didn't wait inside the cab. She climbed right out, then leaned back inside. "You coming in for coffee?"

The blood heated in my veins, and my mouth instantly went dry. The last time she had invited me in for coffee...I...we...had wine. No. I didn't mean to write that. I meant to say—the last time she invited me in for coffee, we had kissed, had become intimate, had nearly had sex on her sofa. Was I ready for that? I mean, Abbie had said, "If it is just sex, then it's just sex," but it wouldn't be just sex with Emily. It couldn't. It would be so much more.

"I won't bite."

A part of me hoped that she would. I gave her a smile and nodded, shutting down the engine. I hadn't even been aware I could multitask. Amazing what the right woman can do for you.

Emily had moved to my side of the cab and held out her hand. As I took it, I felt the familiar jolt between us and gripped hold of her fingers as she led me to her house.

She went through to the kitchen and started filling the kettle whilst I stood in the doorway, watching every move she made. I didn't want coffee; I didn't want wine; I wanted her. Her, and only her. It didn't seem to me as if I actually moved, but one moment I was in the doorway, the next I was turning her around to face me, my arms wrapping around her neck. Staring into her eyes, I knew I'd made the right decision. They were filled with the same thing mine were surely showing. Desire. The desire for each other.

This time the kiss wasn't chaste, or soft, or tender; it was a claiming. This time it held nothing back. This time it promised forever.

My hands slipped into her hair and gripped, pulling her to me in the process.

Her arms circled my waist, and then her hands slid up my back.

Our bodies were moulded against one another, but it wasn't enough. I wanted more.

Breaking away from the kiss, I murmured, "Emily?"

It was all that she needed.

"Come."

She led me towards the stairs, stopping frequently to return to my mouth time and time again. Her hands moved over the buttons of my shirt, popping each one until the material flapped to the side. Emily drew back and looked at me, her eyelids hooded with apparent desire. A slender finger traced the curve of my breast, eliciting a moan from me. She cupped my breast with her palm and squeezed with just the right amount of pressure. My nipples were erect and ready for her, and the sensation of her holding me was almost too much to bear. I could feel the nipple straining to touch her through the silkiness of my bra, and I covered her hand with my own and pressed hers closer.

Brown eyes flicked up to meet my intent stare, our breathing ragged. Her lips glistened in the half light, and I had to taste them again, had to capture those tantalizing lips with my own. So I did, crushing her to me and sandwiching her hand between our bodies.

By the time we had reached her bedroom, my shirt was gone. I was trying to unbutton hers, but my hands were not functioning the way I wanted them to. They were trembling, out of my control.

Emily moved my hands aside. "Let me."

I stepped back and watched her pop each button through its small slit with ease. I couldn't tear my eyes away as she slipped the crisp white shirt from her body and exposed strong shoulders, the mound of her breasts, a taut, flat stomach.

My mouth was painfully dry. I reached out for her and trailed a single finger along her collar bone, then that finger dipped, progressed down her cleavage and over her stomach. I could feel the muscles twitching, could hear her breathing becoming laboured. When I touched cool metal, I realised I was at the button of her trousers. I looked up, into her eyes, and saw her eyebrow lift slightly. Pop. Open. Then the zipper, slowly, so slowly, moved downwards.

This wasn't like our fevered encounter on the sofa. Oh, I wanted her; God, I wanted her, but this wasn't a frenzied satisfying of need like before; it wasn't a fumble. This was so much more.

I tugged gently at the material and was surprised when the trousers readily dropped to the floor. She stepped out of them and kicked them to the side in one motion, leaving her in only her bra and panties.

I stepped back to drink her in. Emily Carson was beyond beautiful, and if I could ever find the words to express just how beautiful, I would undoubtedly be classed as a genius.

The light from the hallway cast a shadow over one side of her face. This was what desire looked like, and it was addictive. I quickly removed my shoes and trousers and stepped close to her. My hands caressed her stomach, and then slid up to cup her breasts. Soft, firm, pliable. The feel of her breasts against my hands was indescribable. Her nipples grazed against my palms as I gently squeezed. Her hands were behind my back, unclipping my bra. The straps fell down my arms, and the bra joined the clothing we were leaving in our wake.

I toyed with the lace hem of her panties before slipping the silky material down strong, muscular thighs. I knelt in front of her and kissed each thigh in turn, then slowly moved upwards, encouraged by the sounds she was making, exhilarated by the way her fingers were moving through my hair.

The pure scent of her was like a drug, and my mouth was watering in anticipation. God. She smelled so fucking good. Spreading her thighs, I dipped my mouth to her most secret place and gently kissed her. She moaned. Another kiss, and then I had to dip inside. With a slight push, my tongue parted her and I reached the wetness. The taste drove me to bury my face completely into the heat of her and delight in her exquisite essence. Strong fingers grasped my hair and pushed me in harder. She said my name over and over as I feasted from her, deeper and deeper, my hands pulling her impossibly closer.

As she suddenly stepped back from me, I stumbled forward, my eyes blinking open in surprise. Had she changed her mind? Didn't she want me as much as I wanted her?

Strong hands slipped under my arms and pulled me to my feet. Hot lips claimed mine. All expectation of taking our time was abandoned when she growled into my mouth. She turned and guided me backwards towards the bed. No sooner was I was lying down than she was on top of me, her hands scrabbling at my underwear. When they were gone, Emily used her knees to part me, slipped her body between my legs and pressed her mound against mine. Another push, another groan; her mouth capturing mine. I gripped her ass and pulled her into me, luxuriating in the contact of her whole body against mine, loving the wetness from her that was mixing with my own with each movement.

I needed her inside me, needed to feel her fingers slip between my legs and part me, slip along the shaft of me, move towards my opening and fill me.

Emily was trembling, and I knew it was with desire and not fear. She was trying to slow it down, trying to make our first time perfect and slow and tender, but both of us were too far gone for that.

I needed to feel the power of her as she plunged inside; watch her eyes full of want as she looked into my own as she fucked me hard, as she took me and made me hers.

Lifting my knees opened me wider for her, invited her inside.

Emily pulled her face away from mine and leaned back from me. Her hands moved down my body in a caress, until her fingers dipped between my legs and reached the place where I needed her to be. She tilted her head, as if asking for permission, and I answered her with a thrust of my hips.

Instead of entering me, she slipped over my wetness, teasing my clit on the way. One eyebrow raised, she gave me the half smile I loved so much. She lowered her head, captured a nipple in her mouth and sucked. I bucked against her, and her fingers almost slipped inside. But no. She moved them away and continued to tease my clit with her thumb whilst laving my breast with her mouth. I thrust again, hoping she would take pity on me, hoping she would bring me to release. Again she flicked her fingers near my entrance but refused to enter.

A smile crossed my face. Two could play at that game. With one movement, she was on her back and I was straddling her. Brown eyes looked surprised. I grabbed her hands and pinned them to her sides before moving my mouth down her body, purposely missing her breasts. Emily groaned and tried to guide me back, but I held her wrists tightly.

I was back where I wanted to be, back at the apex of her and ready to finish what I'd started. Looking up, I saw Emily gazing down at me, her expression expectant. A slight puff of air from my lips cooled her wetness, and I felt her squirm against me. I grinned at her as I lowered my face, never breaking eye contact. Again I dipped my tongue into the crease of her; I pushed it down and then dragged it back.

"God!"

Emily's eyelids fluttered, but she kept her gaze upon me. A flick elicited a gasp and a jerk of her hips, my name tumbling from her.

I opened my mouth and captured her fully, then used my tongue to tease the hard nub. I let her hands escape from mine, and they slipped into my hair and pulled me into her. Her scent was addictive, gloriously addictive, and I felt as if I was falling into her. With a grip on her thighs, I opened her wider and nuzzled more deeply into her. I could feel her opening teasing me, and I knew I had to be inside. Circling, slowly circling her was an agony. Emily was trying to speak, but words were lost on me...lost on her, as the words came out as mumbles.

In. Slow and sure. I waited inside her before flicking the tip of my tongue. I loved the way she ground her hips into my face. The taste of her on the inside was even more wonderful, although that likely was more to do with actually being inside of her than the taste.

Out. And left her wanting.

In. Even deeper.

Out. To take a breath.

The rhythm of taking her was enhanced by the movement of her hips, her groin, her legs pushing into the mattress.

"More. Please, Elles. More. I need more of you."

Two fingers replaced my tongue, and I slipped them inside her; her walls rewarding them with a welcoming spasm. I slowly retracted my fingers, then pushed them in with more force. I wanted to continue devouring her while I was taking her with my fingers, but Emily pulled me up her body for a kiss, thus pushing my fingers deeper inside her. Our bodies moved in unison, sweat slicking our skin and enabling our bodies to slip effortlessly against one another. She was so wet, so fucking wet. The heat poured from her, and I was totally under her spell as she pulsed around my fingers.

When I pulled out of her, I felt her body lift toward my hand, but she stilled as I returned with three fingers hovering outside her entrance. I didn't have time to ask permission. Emily grabbed my wrist and pushed the three digits deep inside.

"God! Yes!"

Her hands tugged, gripped, pulled me closer whilst I took Emily, claimed her, made her mine, made us one. I used my hips to push my hand in more deeply and gloried in the noises she made. My movement became faster, and I delved deeper, the rhythm pulsing, the need to feel her cum overriding everything else. We were so close, almost melting into one another. Her hands gripped my ass and pulled me down hard, almost crushing my hand in the process. I didn't care. I was beyond caring about anything but her, beyond anything but loving her. Loving her. Lov-ing her.

"I love you, Emily."

No sooner had the words had left my mouth than she came, coating my hand with her innermost nectar. An almost primal scream changed into words of loving me too.

Seeing her head thrown back, the muscles of her neck straining, nearly made me join her in the blinding, searing light and place of wonder. But I couldn't. Or I didn't want to. I was too mesmerised by her; too mesmerised by my admission of love, by her mumbled declaration. Was it just a spur of the moment thing that had made words of love appear? Or maybe it was because of the orgasm. For her, not for me.

My fingers were still deep inside her, and I could feel the aftershocks of her orgasm pulsing against my fingers as I kissed my way up her stomach. I stopped to capture a nipple and suck it into my mouth. Emily was stroking my back, my hair, the side of my face, and I knew she was looking at me. Lifting my gaze, I released her nipple and rested my chin on her chest to stare back at her adoringly.

"I love you so much, Ellie. So much." She spoke softly, but with intensity. Her thumb brushed over my eyebrow making me flutter my eyes. "I think I fell in love with you the very first time I saw you with Charlie."

I frowned as I thought of our first meeting, when she had attacked me to get Charlie's ball back. That certainly wasn't the action of someone who had fallen for someone. Other than literally. But that had changed. My frown turned into a smile.

"I knew that someone who could love him as much as I did was a special kind of woman— a woman who loves truthfully and with everything she is." Emily leaned forward and kissed my brow. "And I was right."

How could she say that? I'd spent so long being bitter about love and life, there was no way she could've seen such positive attributes in me when we first met. A lump of emotion lodged in my throat and kept me from replying.

Emily laughed as she pinned me with her gorgeous eyes. "You think you're a tough one, Anderson, but..." With one fluid movement I was on my back, my fingers pulled from inside her. "You...are...as...soft as butter."

Her voice was a growl, and I felt expectation flood through me. Her mouth captured mine, and thoughts of anything but that moment were lost.

I wrapped my legs around her and felt myself lifted up off the bed before being pushed back into the mattress. Her lips were on my throat, blazing a trail of kisses and nips along my sensitive skin. God, Emily felt good. This felt good. Everything felt wonderfully good. But I needed more. Needed her to take me and make me hers, love me from the outside in and the inside out.

There was no hesitation in her entry. Brown eyes locked onto mine and she was within my inner sanctum, her lips moving as if she meant to speak, but no words came out. She was so deep inside, so deep, but her fingers were still. It seemed as if she was waiting for me to be ready for her, but I was more than ready. I'd been ready for her for so long. Emily pulled out, then plunged back inside. When she curled her fingers, it made me gasp. I wanted to hold her there, keep her imprisoned inside. I wanted to know she was always going to be with me.

The tempo was increasing, the urgency of each thrust a sweet agony of want. Her hair was trailing across my skin, teasing my flesh into goose bumps. Emily grabbed my hand and placed it on the side of her face. She hovered directly above me, her mouth so close and yet impossible to reach, brown eyes focused on mine as she took me. I clutched her fingers, and she used my own strength to plunge deeper, take me harder, own me.

Sweat facilitated the movement; lust increased the speed. I could feel my nails digging into the skin on her hand and her back. Emily pushed harder, plunged even more deeply. Our breathing was erratic, laboured; our coupling frenetic, wild, primitively perfect. We were making noises—grunts and half-formed words. I could feel the burn of that elusive sensation, that joyous tingle of my cumming tearing through me to complete me.

I came, gasping my love for Emily into her mouth, hot delirious kisses sealing our joining. I felt her tense an instant before she came for a second time, and as the aftershocks of orgasm charged through me, my body quivered and spasmed with bliss. Kisses slowed, but were still steeped in heat and longing. Mouth captured mouth, and hands were free to explore the curves and slickness of satisfied bodies.

I felt the wetness on my lashes as I opened my eyes to look at Emily. I don't know why the tears were there, as I felt the most loved I had ever felt in my life. Happiness, I suppose. A feeling I would be having all the time, now that I had Emily in my life.

We made love all night, and each time was as perfect as the first. Loving her, taking her, tasting and pleasuring her... I'd never felt this way about anyone in my life, and I knew with certainty that my feelings for her would never change. She was etched into my skin, every layer. Her soul was somehow connected to mine; being without her was inconceivable. She was mine as much as I was hers. It was meant to be. Each kiss, stroke, caress, and look told me so. I loved her, and she loved me. That's all that mattered.

✿

It was the latest I'd woken in a month and I was content, happy with my life. My head was nestled on Emily's chest, and I could feel her steady breathing as she slept. Tracing a path from her collar bone, I took the opportunity to see her naked in the morning light. She was more breath taking than I could comprehend, and I gently kissed the curve of one breast.

She mumbled something and nestled her jaw on top of my head, then wrapped her arm more tightly around me and held me close.

I could see faint bruising on her skin and blushed at the memory of the previous night. Emily Carson had definitely made me hers...that I could say. I hoped she felt the same way this morning.

Ping. Seed of doubt time.

Would she feel the same way? Was I enough for her? Was last night actually all that it seemed, or was it just what I hoped it had been? She had told me she loved me, even explained her reasons, but what if now, in the bright light of the day, she saw the real me? The one my parents thought was a low-life, a degenerate. A flicker of despair ignited my fears, and I had the urge to flee.

"I love you, Ellie."

It was as if she had heard my thoughts. It was perfect, and I felt myself relaxing into her again. Her hand slipped down my back, and I felt a spark of desire. I was surprised; I had thought we had exhausted ourselves the night before.

Emily's brown eyes were open and looking intently into my face. Lowering her mouth, she kissed me tenderly and that spark exploded into a full-fledged burn. Emily deepened the kiss. It was still gentle, but it held that element of decision.

Then she was over me, her leg thrown over mine, her mound pressing against my thigh. She began to move, slowly, her lips still on mine, her body covering me. I lifted my thigh to press into her, while my other leg curled around her and increased the pressure. Our lips separated, and we just stared into each other's eyes as we moved against one another.

This wasn't sex. This was love. We were making love. Gently. Urgently gently. Our eyes fixed on each other's, our hearts in our throats ready to explode with our consummation. There was no need for fingers or tongues; all we needed was each other and the intimate contact between two lovers.

When we came, we came as one. Our hearts, our minds, our everything. We didn't break eye contact, just shuddered our release into the gap separating our mouths before a kiss sealed it all.

Perfect. So perfect. Just like her.

At ten-thirty, we were at the Dogs Trust, a new lead and red ball in hand.

Charlie was waiting for us when we arrived, as if he knew we would be early today, as if he knew today was the first day of the rest of his life. I wondered if he knew it felt the same for me. Probably. He was one smart lad.

I clicked his lead to his collar, and Charlie moved in the opposite direction from his usual walk out the back of the kennels. He made his way to the front entrance, the entrance where we had parked my truck. Amazingly, he knew which vehicle was mine even before I led him towards it. He didn't bat an eyelid when I opened the dog carrier I had on the back seat. He happily scrambled up to take his place on his new blanket and bed.

"Looks like someone knows his way home." Charlie's key worker, Sharon, laughed as she leaned inside the box and patted him lovingly on the head. "You've got two mummies now, fella."

How did she know? I turned to look at Emily, who was smiling at me with such love on her face, Sharon would have been an idiot to miss it.

"Good to see you two worked out your differences. Charlie needs all the love he can get."

She needn't worry. He would have enough love to last him a lifetime. That was one thing I was sure of.

Epilogue

It has been over seven months since the day we collected our little man from the Trust, and each day has been an experience. Mostly good. We won't mention the digging up of my favourite plant. No. Not by Charlie. Emily. She thought it was a weed. Emily and I are stronger than ever. Life with her is *nearly* perfect. The only downside to our love is living separately, but that is soon to change. No. I'm not moving into her house, and she isn't moving into mine. We are buying a house together, complete with a huge garden and lots of potential. In other words, it needs work—something that doesn't scare either of us. A landscape gardener and a property developer should do fine, shouldn't they?

When I started this tale, I mentioned the very first time I fell in love. Now you know I was lying, don't you? I'd skipped over Toby—probably just to get your attention, as I didn't want this story to be full of my grief for my first and lost love. Don't get me wrong, Toby is still in here, still wedged inside my heart, but now I can bring up his memory without experiencing the agony of him being gone. What I was hoping to show you is a progression: love blossoming, and how I overcame my grief, my anger, my aversion to letting love inside again.

My parents still hate me. That is something they need to deal with, not me. If they can't accept who I am, who I love, then do I really want, or need, them in my life? No.

One thing I have learned is that we have to be who we are and not who others want us to be. I didn't set out to be gay, didn't set out planning to go against their wishes. This is who I am: Ellie Anderson, Lesbian.

Being gay doesn't define me, either. Does Charlie love me any less if I am gay rather than straight? Rich or poor? No. He loves me for who I am. Maybe one day, people will take a leaf out of his book and overlook age, size, intellect, religion, sexual orientation, disability, skin colour, and anything else that doesn't sit right with the "perfect people" in this big diverse world in which we live.

It was true that I wasn't looking for love, never intended to fall so completely under the spell of that gorgeous boy. It is also true that I didn't fight the feelings I had for Charlie. So, why did I fight what I felt for Emily? Was it really because I believed I couldn't have one without losing the other? Or was it plain old fear of opening myself up to being hurt again?

Losing someone you love is devastating, whether they be animal or human. The grief comes in waves and takes you by surprise just when you think you are doing fine. Nothing can prepare us for that. There are no classes you can attend that can help you prepare for loss, and loss comes in many shapes and sizes. Losing the love of my parents hurt. It was like a kick in the teeth. But I couldn't, and never will, lose who I am inside. To that, I will be true, and I hope you will be too.

Charlie loved us from the start, he trusted from the start, and look what he had endured—beatings, injuries, abandonment. And I thought I'd had it rough. He didn't let the past impinge on what he could have; he didn't let the actions of one bastard hold him back from what he wanted. And what did he want? Love. Acceptance. A ball, and someone to throw it for him. He wanted a world where he could play and be happy.

Not really a lot to ask for when you think about it. Love is free and should be given freely, whether by man or dog.

When I consider the events that led me to Emily, it still makes me smile to think that Abbie did make a match after all, but I forgive her. Who wouldn't? She's my sister, and only did what she did for my sake. If it hadn't been for her going to the Trust on New Year's Day, I would never have met Charlie, never have met Emily. That would mean I would still be the same as I was in 2011—a bitter and twisted old lezza with a penchant for Hebe.

I'm coming to the end of my rambling now, as I have to meet with Abbie, Rob, Lils, and Poppy. Emily is outside playing with Charlie. His excited woofs are drifting in from outside. It is family time, a time we should cherish. And I do. Very much. I make sure all the people in my life know how much they mean to me each and every day, whether through my actions or my words. Knowing they know I love them is what truly matters.

Now I am contemplating how to finish this story. Should I just write "The End" and scuttle off somewhere, or should I try to pass on a little more of what I have learned?

You guessed it.

Ice cream and nuts. You can have both, and don't let anyone tell you differently. Emily is my ice cream, and I am nuts about her. Sorted.

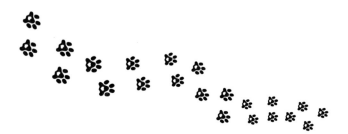

About L.T. Smith

L.T. is a late bloomer when it comes to writing and didn't begin until 2005 with her first novel *Hearts and Flowers Border* (first published in 2006).

She soon caught the bug and has written numerous tales, usually with a comical slant to reflect, as she calls it, "My warped view of the dramatic."

Although she loves to write, L.T. loves to read, too—being an English teacher seems to demand it. Most of her free time is spent with her furry little men—two fluffy balls of trouble who keep her active and her apologies flowing.

Facebook: https://www.facebook.com/LT-Smith
E-mail her at fingersmith@hotmail.co.uk

St. Hubert's Animal Welfare Center, USA

For those not able or not wanting to donate to the Dogs Trust—you might want to consider St. Hubert's Animal Welfare Center:

Founded in 1939, St. Hubert's Animal Welfare Center is a nonprofit 501 (c)(3) organization dedicated to the humane treatment of companion animals. The organization believes in and provides services that support the human-animal bond and seeks to foster an environment in which people respect all loving creatures. Its services to the community include pet adoption and animal rescue; humane education, dog training, and professional education; and pet loss support. St. Hubert's has shelters in Madison and North Branch, NJ, and a Behavior and Training Center in Madison. Shelters are open seven days a week. Visit them at www.sthuberts.org

Other books from Ylva Publishing

http://www.ylva-publishing.com

See Right Through Me

L.T. Smith

ISBN: 978-3-95533-068-2
Length: 310 pages

Trust, respect, and love. Three little words—that's all. But these words are powerful, and if we ignore any one of them, then three other little words take their place: jealousy, insecurity, and heartbreak.

Schoolteacher Gemma Hughes is an ordinary woman living an ordinary life. Disorganised and clumsy, she soon finds herself in the capable hands of the beautiful Dr Maria Moran. Everything goes wonderfully until Gemma starts doubting Maria's intentions and begins listening to the wrong people.

But has Maria something to hide, or is it a case of swapping trust for insecurity, respect for jealousy and finishing with a world of heartbreak and deceit? Can Gemma stop her actions before it's too late? Or will she ruin the best thing to happen in her life?

Given her track record, anything is possible…

Hot Line

Alison Grey

ISBN: 978-3-95533-048-4
Length: 114 pages

Two women from different worlds.

Linda, a successful psychologist, uses her work to distance herself from her own loneliness.

Christina works for a sex hotline to make ends meet.

Their worlds collide when Linda calls Christina's sex line. Christina quickly realizes Linda is not her usual customer. Instead of wanting phone sex, Linda makes an unexpected proposition. Does Christina dare accept the offer that will change both their lives?

L.A. Metro
(second edition)

RJ Nolan

ISBN: 978-3-95533-041-5
Length: 349 pages

Dr. Kimberly Donovan's life is in shambles. After her medical ethics are questioned, first her family, then her closeted lover, the Chief of the ER, betray her. Determined to make a fresh start, she flees to California and L.A. Metropolitan Hospital.

Dr. Jess McKenna, L.A. Metro's Chief of the ER, gives new meaning to the phrase emotionally guarded, but she has her reasons.

When Kim and Jess meet, the attraction is immediate. Emotions Jess has tried to repress for years surface. But her interest in Kim also stirs dark memories. They settle for friendship, determined not to repeat past mistakes, but secretly they both wish things could be different.

Will the demons from Jess's past destroy their future before it can even get started? Or will L.A. Metro be a place to not only heal the sick, but to mend wounded hearts?

Something in the Wine

Jae

ISBN: 978-3-95533-005-7
Length: 393 pages

All her life, Annie Prideaux has suffered through her brother's constant practical jokes only he thinks are funny. But Jake's last joke is one too many, she decides when he sets her up on a blind date with his friend Drew Corbin—neglecting to tell his straight sister one tiny detail: her date is not a man, but a lesbian.

Annie and Drew decide it's time to turn the tables on Jake by pretending to fall in love with each other.

At first glance, they have nothing in common. Disillusioned with love, Annie focuses on books, her cat, and her work as an accountant while Drew, more confident and outgoing, owns a dog and spends most of her time working in her beloved vineyard.

Only their common goal to take revenge on Jake unites them. But what starts as a table-turning game soon turns Annie's and Drew's lives upside down as the lines between pretending and reality begin to blur.

Something in the Wine is a story about love, friendship, and coming to terms with what it means to be yourself.

Broken Faith
(revised edition)

Lois Cloarec Hart

ISBN: 978-3-95533-056-9
Length: 415 pages

Emotional wounds aren't always apparent, and those that haunt Marika and Rhiannon are deep and lasting.

On the surface, Marika appears to be a wealthy, successful lawyer, while Rhiannon is a reclusive, maladjusted loner. But Marika, in her own way, is as damaged as the younger Rhiannon. When circumstances throw them together one summer, they begin to reach out, each finding unexpected strengths in the other.

However, even as inner demons are gradually vanquished and old hurts begin to heal, evil in human form reappears. The cruelly enigmatic Cass has used and controlled Marika in the past, and she aims to do so again.

Can Marika find it within herself to break free? Can she save her young friend from Cass' malevolent web? With the support of remarkable friends, the pair fights to break free—of their crippling pasts and the woman who will own them or kill them.

Coming from Ylva Publishing in spring 2014

http://www.ylva-publishing.com

Coming Home
(revised edition)

Lois Cloarec Hart

A triangle with a twist, Coming Home is the story of three good people caught up in an impossible situation.

Rob, a charismatic ex-fighter pilot severely disabled with MS, has been steadfastly cared for by his wife, Jan, for many years. Quite by accident one day, Terry, a young writer/postal carrier, enters their life and turns it upside down.

Injecting joy and turbulence into their quiet existence, Terry draws Rob and Jan into her lively circle of family and friends until the growing attachment between the two women begins to strain the bonds of love and loyalty, to Rob and each other.

Hearts and Flowers Border
(revised edition)

L.T. Smith

A visitor from her past jolts Laura Stewart into memories—some funny, some heart-wrenching. Thirteen years ago, Laura buried those memories so deeply she never believed they would resurface. Still, the pain of first love mars Laura's present life and might even destroy her chance of happiness with the beautiful, yet seemingly unobtainable Emma Jenkins.

Can Laura let go of the past, or will she make the same mistakes all over again?

Hearts and Flowers Border is a simple tale of the uncertainty of youth and the first flush of love—love that may have a chance after all.

In a Heartbeat

RJ Nolan

Veteran police officer Sam McKenna has no trouble facing down criminals on a daily basis but breaks out in a sweat at the mere mention of commitment. A recent failed relationship strengthens her resolve to stick with her trademark no-strings-attached affairs.

Dr. Riley Connolly, a successful trauma surgeon, has spent her whole life trying to measure up to her family's expectations. And that includes hiding her sexuality from them.

When a routine call sends Sam to the hospital where Riley works, the two women are hurtled into a life-and-death situation. The incident binds them together. But can there be any future for a commitment-phobic cop and a closeted, workaholic doctor?

Puppy Love
© by L.T. Smith

ISBN 978-3-95533-144-3

Also available as e-book.

Published by Ylva Publishing, legal entity of Ylva Verlag, e.Kfr.

Ylva Verlag, e.Kfr.
Owner: Astrid Ohletz
Am Kirschgarten 2
65830 Kriftel
Germany

http://www.ylva-publishing.com

First edition: November 2013

Credits:
Edited by Day Petersen
Cover Design by Amanda Chron

Lightning Source UK Ltd.
Milton Keynes UK
UKOW03f0044310514

232627UK00001B/3/P